LET THE BATTLE BEGIN

This edition published in 2017 by Paper Rocket
an imprint of Parragon Books Ltd.
Paper Rocket logo and name ™ Parragon Books Ltd

Parragon Books Ltd
Chartist House
15–17 Trim Street
Bath BA1 1HA, UK
www.parragon.com

Story by Craig Kyle & Christopher Yost and Stephany Folsom and Eric Pearson
Screenplay by Eric Pearson
Adapted by Jim McCann
Before the Battle (Bridge Story) by Steve Behling
Directed by Taika Waititi
Produced by Kevin Feige

ISBN 978-1-4748-8325-2

Printed in UK

MARVEL
THOR RAGNAROK
LET THE BATTLE BEGIN

PAPER ROCKET
Stories that take you to another world

BEFORE THE BATTLE

PROLOGUE

Before.

The Battle of New York.

An invading force of otherworldly Chitauri warriors had flooded the city. Destruction followed in their wake. There seemed to be no stopping them. That's what most people thought, including the World Security Council. In an effort to contain the invasion and end it before it could spread across the world, the World Security Council was ready to give the order: nuke New York.

It's quite possible that the city, and the rest of the world, would have fallen to the Chitauri. But it wouldn't have been because of the World Security Council's attempt to blow New York City off the map. That never happened. No, the turning of the tide came down to a team of six individuals, known collectively as the Avengers.

Two of those individuals were at present riding atop a great Chitauri beast that careened through the concrete canyons of the city. Thor and the Hulk fought side by side, comrades-in-arms, delivering blow after blow to the oncoming Chitauri. The warriors flung themselves at the heroes in an effort to destroy them utterly.

Pity for them it didn't work.

The two Avengers fought together in silence. Thor slammed the Chitauri with his enchanted hammer, Mjolnir. Hulk smashed the Chitauri with his non-enchanted, huge, very hard fists. Both did the job quite nicely.

They didn't know what damage the Chitauri beast could cause if it escaped their grasp, and they didn't want to find out. The Hulk prised a hunk of the creature's metal hide from its body, heaved it over his head, and hurled it straight down. Seeing this, Thor turned his attention from the Chitauri warriors, and drove his hammer into the hole that Hulk had made. But he wasn't just *striking* the beast. Alone, the blow that Thor delivered would not have stopped the alien.

No. It was Thor's mighty hammer Mjolnir that summoned lightning from the sky, delivering a terminal jolt to the massive monster.

An unearthly sound erupted from deep within the creature as it lost all control. One moment it had been soaring above the streets of Manhattan. The next, it was heading on a collision course for New York's famed Grand Central Station. The beast smashed through solid concrete, stone, metal and glass, shattering it to pieces, as it came screeching to a halt in the middle of the now empty commuter hub.

Hulk and Thor held on, riding the Chitauri beast to the ground.

They were victorious.

Each took a brief moment to catch his breath, as debris from Grand Central Station piled around them. Thor surveyed the felled beast, satisfied that the two Avengers had done their job. He nodded slightly, as if to say, We have fought well, my friend.

Hulk punched Thor in the head.

It was that kind of friendship.

CHAPTER 1

When one thinks of the Hulk, the first thing that comes to one's mind is probably big green angry guy who flies an Avengers Quinjet.

Wait. That's not the first thing that comes to mind?

Well, then you must not know Hulk.

Just a few moments ago, the Hulk had been standing on the surface of a S.H.I.E.L.D. (Strategic Homeland Intervention, Enforcement and Logistics Division) Helicarrier – pretty much, as its name suggests, a flying aircraft carrier. The Helicarrier served as a mobile headquarters for S.H.I.E.L.D. The Hulk was on board for only a moment, just long enough to deposit Natasha

Romanoff – Black Widow – on its expansive deck.

Hulk, along with the rest of the Avengers, had been locked in a life-or-death struggle against an incredible artificial intelligence named Ultron. That the Hulk – Bruce Banner, actually – had a hand in Ultron's creation was lost neither on Banner nor his green-skinned alter ego. For unbeknownst to the rest of the Avengers, Banner and Tony Stark had been working in secret to develop a defence system that could protect the Earth from almost any threat, including alien invasion. A system that, somewhat ironically, had proved in and of itself to be one of the greatest threats Earth had ever faced.

It had been Tony Stark's dream, to be fair. He wanted to leave a legacy, something that would make everyone safe. The secret to this defence system – dubbed Ultron – was its artificial intelligence. The secret to creating this artificial intelligence had eluded both Stark and Banner. But the dream appeared to be within their grasp when Stark obtained a strange gem taken from a sceptre that belonged to Loki – adopted brother to the mighty Thor. The gem made the seemingly impossible happen. Ultron came to life.

As often happens to the best-laid plans of mice and men, however, something went wrong. As Ultron sprang to sentient life, it decided that the biggest threat facing the planet was humanity itself. It took the combined might of every Avenger – Hulk, Black Widow, Iron Man, Thor, Captain America and Hawkeye – plus the help of two super-powered individuals, Wanda and Pietro Maximoff, and the aid of a synthetic human known as Vision, to stop Ultron and his vast robot army.

The Hulk had channelled his anger and rage for a just cause, once again saving the people of Earth from a terrible fate. In the process, however, he – Banner – came to realize that the Earth also needed to be saved ... from him. Before the final battle with Ultron, the Hulk had been driven into a dangerous rampage by Wanda. She and her brother had briefly allied themselves with Ultron, before they understood what the artificial intelligence had planned for humanity. Wanda's powers had caused the Hulk to suffer awful hallucinations. The hallucinations pushed Hulk to the brink, and he was on the verge of becoming the monster that some truly believed him to be. Only Tony Stark, wearing an anti-Hulk suit made of Iron Man armour, was able to stop the Hulk.

And only Black Widow could help calm the Hulk down, triggering the incredible transformation back from brute to introverted scientist.

Black Widow.

The Hulk – Banner – cared for her. For Natasha Romanoff. Perhaps too much. Certainly enough that he realized she wasn't safe around him. Not while he could turn into an out-of-control creature again. Who knows what might have happened if Stark hadn't been around to subdue the Hulk? Who might have been hurt?

It was this bleak realization that drove the Hulk to his next act. After setting Black Widow gently on to the Helicarrier deck, he turned and looked one last time into his friend's eyes. A voice inside him – Banner's voice – wanted Hulk to linger for just another moment, so he could see her face a little longer.

But the Hulk knew it was time to go. He looked up into the sky as an Avengers Quinjet soared overhead.

Gamma-irradiated leg muscles tensed, then released, sending the Incredible Hulk into the air like a missile. To any human eye, it would have looked like the man-monster was flying. For all intents and purposes, he was. He had hurled himself in the direction of the Quinjet. Such was his speed that he quickly caught up with the craft. The Quinjet's rear bay was open, and the Hulk landed inside with a loud thump, causing the Quinjet to veer suddenly before recovering.

The Hulk grunted and stomped inside. He was unsurprised to find Ultron at the controls. The robot had transferred his artificial intelligence into another Ultron body and was using the Avengers' own transport as a means of escape.

Right after he had tried to destroy the Hulk.

Right after he had tried to destroy the Hulk's friends.

This made the Hulk angry.

"Oh, for God's sake," Ultron said, his robotic voice full of frustration, as the Hulk grabbed his metal body. With another grunt and seemingly little effort, the Hulk hurled Ultron out of the Quinjet's open bay. The robot was helpless against the Hulk's extreme power. It looked like a harmless speck of dust as it fell through empty air to its fate below. Hulk had no idea what would happen to Ultron when it crashed back on Earth. He did know this: a fall from that height would damage Ultron's body beyond repair. He also knew that the Avengers would find what was left of it and shut it down for good.

The Hulk drew a deep breath into his mammoth lungs, held it, and exhaled. Then he heard a voice.

Her voice.

"Hey, big guy, we did it."

Black Widow. Her voice and face came in loud and

clear over a Quinjet monitor. The Hulk walked slowly towards the front of the vehicle, staring at Black Widow as she spoke.

"The job is finished," she continued. Her voice cracked with emotion. "Now I need you to turn this bird round, okay?"

He could have spoken at any moment, even grunted to acknowledge that he'd heard her. Anything to let her know that he was fine, and that he would listen and come back to his team.

But that wasn't on the cards. Not today. From inside the Hulk, Banner knew he had to get away. As long as he could transform into the rampaging Hulk, no one would be safe around him – least of all his friends.

"We can't track you in stealth mode," Black Widow said. That was true. The Quinjets were capable of travelling almost anywhere without being followed. "So help me out."

The Hulk stared at the image of Black Widow on the screen. She looked tired from the battle with Ultron. Most of all, she looked concerned for her friend. The Hulk sensed this, and reached out to the screen, like he was going to touch her hand.

"I need y–"

The Hulk gently pressed a button on the monitor, cutting off Black Widow midsentence.

Alone, the Hulk sat on the floor of the Quinjet as its engines whined, the automatic controls sending the mighty ship through the Earth's upper atmosphere and into the deep unknown of space.

CHAPTER 2

One does not simply walk into the Realm of Fire.

Unless the one in question is the son of Odin. In that case, one simply does walk into the Realm of Fire.

Of course, there are consequences that go with so rash a decision.

"Perhaps if they called this 'The Realm of Eternal Summer'," Thor muttered to himself, "they might have more visitors." Thor grinned. He wished someone, anyone, had been around to hear what he had said. He was sure they would have laughed. After all, Thor was quite amusing, if he did say so himself.

But there wasn't much laughter to be found here in the Realm of Fire.

Among Asgardians, it was more commonly referred to as Muspelheim, one of the Nine Realms. It was a land like nothing else. A world of eternal, ever-burning flame, where heat reigned. Water was not to be found on Muspelheim, not anywhere – in its place, bubbling pools of lava dotted the rocky landscape. The skies were rife with the stench of sulphur, and minute particles of ash constantly blew in the hot winds.

A holiday spot Muspelheim was not.

How Thor had come to be at Muspelheim was ... what did Earth people like to say? It was ... complicated. For the last few years, the son of Odin had been splitting his time between the realm of Asgard – his home – and Midgard. You might know it as Earth. On that world, Thor had found a sense of responsibility that had eluded him in Asgard. A responsibility to help people, those who could not otherwise help themselves. He had also found friendship and comrades in the form of the Avengers.

It would not be so bad having them for company right now, thought Thor, as he plodded along the searing soil of Muspelheim. He pulled at his beard, now grown long. His garments were worn, tattered. The Thor who walked into Muspelheim was not the same polished Thor who had joined the Avengers.

The Avengers. It had been some time since Thor had fought beside his teammates. The last challenge they had faced was Ultron. The android had an agenda of extinction that it had attempted to force upon the Earth. Alongside his teammates, Thor had fought with valour befitting an Asgardian, shattering Ultron's plans once and for all.

In the middle of that epic battle, however, there had been the vision.

On the surface, the vision seemed to have been caused by Wanda Maximoff — she whose powers could cause a person to have incredibly realistic, disturbing hallucinations. But there was something so vivid, so real about the vision that had come to Thor — something so hellish and frightening that it disturbed him to his very core. He could not, would not believe that the vision was solely the result of another's hallucinatory powers.

In that vision, Thor had glimpsed an eerie room full of Asgardians, his friend Heimdall among them. Heimdall, the so-called Watcher of Worlds, controlled the Bifrost — the bridge that allows beings to travel swiftly from Asgard to the other Realms. Thor had seen Heimdall in this vision, but Heimdall had not seen him — for the Watcher of Worlds was now blind. It was clear that some awful, terrible fate had befallen the Asgardians, but what it was, Thor knew not. For as soon as the vision had come to him, it fled, banished to the shadows of his mind.

But still the vision lingered within Thor. He wondered what it meant. It was not merely a hallucination caused by Wanda. It must have been an ill omen, a portent of something to come. A glimpse into the future of Asgard, a warning to Thor.

Perhaps that explained in part why Thor had made the possibly foolhardy decision to enter Muspelheim alone. Something about the vision had led him to this place. Something that he had seen in his mind's eye, but now could not quite recall. He knew he had to be here, right now. And at least in Muspelheim he would find a welcome distraction. Something to take his mind off the vision. And what better distraction was there than walking through an inhospitable inferno filled with Fire Demons?

He had yet to encounter any Fire Demons, of course, but then, he had only just arrived in this fiery land. It would take the Demons time to realize that an Asgardian had dared enter Muspelheim. Thor wanted, needed a battle – something that would draw his attention to the here and now, allowing him to stay in the moment. He saw not a soul as he trudged along the molten ground. Here he had gone to all the trouble to steal into the Realm of Fire, and no one had come to greet him.

"Unbelievable," Thor said out loud, and he rolled his eyes. So he did what any Asgardian who had just appeared in the flaming world of Muspelheim would do.

He introduced himself.

As only Thor could.

Summoning the power of the storm through his enchanted mallet, Mjolnir, Thor brought down lightning from the sky to meet the scorched earth of the Realm of Fire. He did this repeatedly, causing multiple arcs of pure electricity to strafe the ground.

The sound of the thunder was deafening.

The lightning stopped. Then there was silence.

But only for a moment.

For in the distance, the savage roars of the Fire Demons could be heard. Closer and closer the sound came.

Thor smiled.

CHAPTER 3

"Hulk's head hurts bad," the Hulk muttered unhappily. He rubbed his skull with a thick green hand. His eyes were closed, and yet a bright light burned through his eyelids.

These were the first words the man-monster had uttered in who knows how long. Certainly, they were the first words he had spoken since before he boarded the Quinjet and tossed Ultron to the winds. Before he'd turned off his comm and cut himself off from Black Widow. From anyone on Earth who might find him. Before the Quinjet had taken the Hulk into the depths of space. Before....

Hulk opened his eyes slowly. Harsh sunlight poured in. Quickly, he rose to his feet, still holding his head with one big hand. He took several tentative steps, pounding the ground, and immediately tripped over what looked like a giant old wheel.

For the first time, the Hulk looked round at the landscape around him, and saw that he was standing in what looked like an enormous rubbish dump. As far as he could see, debris was scattered all over the ground. It fell continuously, raining rubbish from the universe all over the desolate ground.

Where was he? Why did his head hurt so much? Why was it so hard to think? Why did Hulk want to think, anyway?

Wait.

Hulk wasn't in the Quinjet? But if Hulk wasn't in the Quinjet, what had happened? Had the vehicle crashed somehow? Had the impact knocked the Hulk unconscious?

Was he back on Earth?

Hulk tried to remember, but that was always difficult for him. Remembering things, like thinking, was more Banner's speed. But somewhere inside the Hulk's clouded brain, there was Banner, wondering, analysing, always the scientist.

The wormhole, Banner thought.

Banner had seen it through the Quinjet's cockpit. He'd known what it was the moment it had appeared there in space, plain as day. It was similar to a black hole, but full of colour. It swirled, brilliant, beckoning. Banner knew it was a wormhole.

The Hulk? He had no idea it was called a wormhole. It was bright and colourful and he didn't like it.

That was unfortunate, because that's exactly where the Quinjet had gone. The Quinjet had burst through the wormhole and somehow deposited the Hulk here, in this strange, unfamiliar place.

The Hulk's head still hurt, and he was tired of Banner, tired of thinking.

The green goliath plodded along the rocky surface crowded with rubbish. The Hulk looked up at the sky, expecting to see the sun that had woken him up so unceremoniously. And there was a sun, to be sure. But there was also something else.

A vast array of swirling lights – like holes in the sky itself.

Wormholes, Banner thought from inside the Hulk's mind.

Hulk grunted in assent as he watched the wormholes swirling in the sky. A steady stream of objects seemed to pour forth from them. He watched intently as all manner of debris escaped the confines of the swirling lights.

Strange crafts, asteroids, satellites and more were being perpetually ejected from the wormholes, falling down to the surface in rapid succession.

"Where Hulk?" he said, his voice bouncing off the dunes and sounding unnaturally loud, even for Hulk.

Banner knew that he was no longer on Earth. Unlike the Hulk, he put two and two together, and realized that the wormhole was a singularity. An interstellar passageway connecting two disparate places. A "space shortcut" between worlds. The Quinjet must have passed through the wormhole and deposited him here. Wherever here was.

"I've got one," came a voice from beyond a piece of metal debris. It looked like a ship of some kind. It was twisted and smoking.... Was it the Quinjet? Hulk couldn't tell for certain. There were so many ships partially covered in the wasteland. It was like some kind of galactic graveyard. "I'll bring him in," said the voice again.

The Hulk curled his upper lip into a savage sneer and grunted. "No one has Hulk," he scowled, and he meant it.

Then he saw her. It was a woman, her head popping over the debris, staring directly at the Hulk. She wore armour, and her arms were bare – Hulk could see she had tattoos of some kind on both. The woman started to walk forward, and as she grew closer, Hulk could see she wore something on her hands that looked like elaborate brass knuckles.

Weapons.

Weapons meant fighting.

Fighting was something the Hulk understood.

An inhuman growl escaped the Hulk's mouth as he bounded towards the woman. Raising his right fist, the goliath brought it down on the spot where the woman stood.

She didn't flinch as the Hulk's fist drove right into the ground in front of her. It was like she had been expecting the Hulk to do exactly that, and stood her ground. The Hulk's momentum carried him through, and he hit the ground, rolling end over end.

This made the Hulk angry.

"Fight," the Hulk snarled.

The woman started to walk forward once more, holding a foblike device in her right hand. "Fight is exactly right," she said. "You're here to fight. The Grandmaster will make sure of that."

She advanced on the Hulk, and the man-monster balled up both fists in anger.

"Leave Hulk alone," Hulk yelled, and he meant it.

"Oh, you'll do nicely," the woman said. "He'll pay me handsomely for what I'm going to bring him."

The Hulk was getting madder by the second, as somewhere deep inside Banner was asking questions. Questions like *Who's the Grandmaster? Who is this woman? What is that thing in her right hand?* But the Hulk had a way of getting Banner to shut up and stop thinking and asking so many questions.

The jade giant clapped his enormous hands together and expected the woman to be blown off her feet by the resulting shock wave. But this did not happen. She hadn't moved even a millimetre. Whoever she was, she had incredible strength.

This both impressed the Hulk and made him really angry.

He threw another punch at the woman, but she easily ducked it. Hulk staggered, thrown off-balance. Turning round, he saw the woman waving the fob in front of his face.

Banner had realized what was going on a while ago – the woman was playing some kind of game with him. She was using the Hulk's anger against him, making him so mad that he kept making mistakes. It was driving the Hulk nuts.

So when the woman waved the fob in the Hulk's face again, the Hulk was sure he had it figured out. He didn't move. He planted his heavy feet in the hot sand and did nothing as he sneered at his foe, daring her to do something.

Which she promptly did.

She activated the fob, and it fired something right at the Hulk's neck. A moment later, the Hulk's muscles tensed, his teeth began to grind uncontrollably, and the worst pain that he'd ever felt coursed through his veins like poison.

And then everything went dark.

CHAPTER 4

"You dare to enter Muspelheim, Asgardian?"

Thor's smile grew wider. The air around him was thick with ash as the first wave of Fire Demons descended, and the son of Odin couldn't have been more pleased. Thor stood his ground, legs braced, brandishing Mjolnir before him. Mjolnir, his enchanted mallet, which had accompanied him into countless battles on countless worlds against countless foes.

The Fire Demon's voice crackled with the sound of an inferno. "None of your kind are welcome in our realm, Asgardian."

"That may be, but I was in the area, and thought I might drop by for a visit," Thor said casually.

The Fire Demons looked at one another, not sure how

to respond. Humour was not a known commodity on Muspelheim. It must have gone up in smoke, along with everything else in the Realm of Fire.

Eventually, the Fire Demon said, "Stay a moment longer and face death. Your own."

"Not this day," Thor shot back. He tightened his grip on Mjolnir.

And just like that, the Fire Demons were upon him.

A battle begins with but a single blow. In this case, it was not Thor who drew first blood, but the Fire Demons.

A single Demon lunged for Thor, its flaming hand gripping his left arm. Thor let out a gasp of pain as the Fire Demon's touch seared his flesh. A sharp blow from Mjolnir dislodged the Fire Demon from his burning arm. Thor clasped a hand over the burn, rubbing it. He clenched his teeth. *That*, he thought, *cannot be allowed to happen again*.

Thor cast a glance at the smouldering ground, focusing on the Fire Demon he had just struck. When he looked up, he saw hundreds more flaming Demons just waiting to attack. He gazed at the horizon, and it was Fire Demons as far as the eye could see.

As he had done so many times before, Thor began to hurl his hammer around his head as fast as he could. The twirling of the mallet kept the Fire Demons at bay, but that was not Thor's true intent. The hammer whirled faster and faster, picking up speed, until at last, Thor released Mjolnir.

Like an arrow, Mjolnir flew straight and true, striking down one Fire Demon after another as it soared away from Thor and into the distance. The Demons struck by Thor's hammer knew defeat that day. But the other Demons were moronic enough to see Thor temporarily deprived of his hammer and think him easy fodder.

Fire Demons could be such fools.

A moment later, Mjolnir returned to Thor's hand. Along the way, it had taken out countless more Fire Demons. Thor reclaimed his enchanted hammer, and looked at the sea of fire before him.

Settle in, he thought to himself, *you're going to be here for a while*.

In the heat of battle, one tends to lose track of things. Since the skirmish with the Fire Demons had begun, Thor had lost track of how long it had been since he had entered

Muspelheim, or how many Fire Demons he had faced. Was it an hour? A day? Fifty Fire Demons? A hundred? More?

Wave after wave of incendiary hordes came upon Thor as he slowly advanced along the molten surface of the Realm of Fire. Each stride brought him closer. Closer to earning the attention of the one Thor had come to see. For he had no interest in the Fire Demons, other than as a diversion.

Mjolnir was in his right hand. Thor let the hammer slide loose, grabbing it by the leather strap that was attached to its grip. He held out his left hand, keeping the Fire Demons away from him even as they continued to advance in droves. Thor twirled the mallet once with incredible force, then released the strap. Mjolnir flew from his hand, colliding with a row of at least fifty Fire Demons. The hammer hit them hard, casting each aside as if they were insignificant ants.

No sooner had the hammer left his hand than it soared back, returning to its master. Thor caught Mjolnir in his right hand and surveyed his work, nodding slightly.

"I'd like to see the Hulk do better," he boasted proudly.

CHAPTER 5

The Hulk was angry, even by Hulk standards.

The thing that had hit him in the neck – whatever it was – hurt. It actually hurt Hulk.

He wasn't used to things hurting, and he really wasn't used to being beaten.

So: angry.

"Hulk's whole body hurts," said the Hulk.

After the horrendous pain, Hulk felt something else he hadn't felt before: paralysed. He couldn't move at all. He kept telling his enormous limbs to move, to smash, but they wouldn't listen. And when the woman strapped some crazy-looking goggles over his head, Hulk couldn't do anything to prevent it. With the goggles on, Hulk couldn't see anything, either.

As the woman took him aboard a vehicle of some kind, he heard a voice come over the communications system. The voice called the woman Scrapper.

So that's who the Hulk was angry at.

Seething, Hulk grunted as he felt the goggles being removed from his face. He could see once again. He reached a hand up to his eyes.

He could also move again.

The Hulk looked around. He was no longer standing in the wasteland, with space junk all around and wormholes swirling in the sky above. Scrapper, the Angry Girl who had somehow, against all odds, subdued him, was nowhere to be seen. No longer was he outside. The Hulk now stood inside what could only be described as a ring.

A fighting ring.

Hulk rubbed his eyes, clearing them. Standing in the ring along with him were five others.

They weren't human.

Then again, was the Hulk really human? Somewhere inside him, Banner wondered.

"Welcome to Sakaar, my friend," came a voice from out of nowhere. It was loud and friendly and Hulk hated it.

"Let's see if you'll make a worthy addition to my Contest of Champions."

The Hulk grunted. Inside, Banner had questions. *What's Sakaar? Is that the name of this place? This planet?*

The five other beings in the ring were just as large and imposing as the Hulk. Some had multiple arms, some multiple legs, and one of them appeared to be made of stone itself.

"Not Hulk's friend," the green behemoth muttered.

"Oh, come now," said the disembodied voice. "I'm everyone's friend. Just ask them! Well, not everyone's. But let's not dwell on that. How about a battle? I'm willing to bet that you're quite good when it comes to fighting. You seem tailor-made for it."

So that's what's going on here, Banner thought from inside the Hulk's mind. *I'm supposed to fight with these ... beings. It's a game of some kind.*

Hulk sneered again, his lip curling in what appeared to be a smile. A fighting game was one he knew how to win.

"What manner of creature is this?!" screamed a four-armed alien as it landed face-first on the ground. A second later, a heavy, wide green foot stepped on its back, causing the four-armed alien to yelp in pain. "Where did you find this thing?!"

From the moment the six-way battle had begun, the Hulk was squarely in his element. To say that he was evenly matched or that this competition was remotely close would have been one big gamma-irradiated lie. The Hulk was absolutely mopping the floor with his competitors. Though each one was roughly his size (or larger), and each one possessed incredible strength, the Hulk was better. He was stronger.

Strongest one there is, thought the Hulk.

The Hulk was like a kid in a sweet shop – he hardly knew which opponent to fight next. They all looked so easy to defeat! A three-metre-tall beast of an alien snarled at the Hulk, thick drool dripping from its fangs. That was all the invitation the Hulk needed.

The green-skinned goliath rammed a fist into the beast's belly, knocking it flat on its behind. The beast yowled in pain, and spat out words in a language the Hulk had never heard before. It sounded like cursing to the Hulk. He didn't like it. So he lifted the four-armed beast over his head, and threw him right into one of his other opponents.

The beast collided with a six-legged insect-like creature, and both went down for the count.

"Fight," commanded the Hulk, as he stared at his remaining opponents. In the heat of battle, a thought occurred to Banner: *Hulk is enjoying this. He's actually enjoying this.*

"Fight!" snarled the Hulk once more. As if in answer, an amorphous orange blob oozed from behind the Hulk, covering him in an instant. For a moment, the Hulk was surprised – he found himself enveloped in a viscous goo, unable to breathe. He tried to punch his way out. But the orange blob stretched with the Hulk's fist as he punched, and snapped back. It clung tight to the Hulk and wouldn't let go.

This really made the Hulk angry.

And so he pounded the floor with both fists. The resulting shock wave caused the ring to shake. Still the orange blob held fast. So the Hulk hit the floor again. And again. And again. The whole room was shaking, and slowly, too, was the orange blob. The vibrations from the Hulk's thunderous blows started to cause breaks in the goo. The Hulk was now able to breathe. He thrust both arms back as fast as he could and threw the orange blob off his body. The creature landed with a loud *THWUCK*.

The Hulk punched it, and the blob splattered into a hundred smaller, inert blobs.

The scaly-skinned creature was next, Hulk decided. For its part, the scaly-skinned creature seemed almost reluctant to fight – it had seen what it was up against, and maybe decided it wasn't exactly worth the effort to get smashed. But there was nothing the creature could do as the Hulk ran directly towards it, his fists knocking the lizard-like being off its feet. Scales sprayed into the air as Hulk knocked the creature back. The alien collapsed, landing in a heap on the floor.

Elapsed time from the start of Hulk's battle to his victory over five alien competitors: two minutes, ten seconds.

The Hulk turned his head from left to right, looking at his fallen competitors. They were all still alive, and all shaking their heads, wondering what – or more precisely, who – had happened to them.

Hulk found himself wishing he had someone else to punch.

Then came a sound. Something unexpected that got Hulk's attention.

It was ... applause. Applause could be heard inside the ring. Hulk jerked his head up, looking around. From out of the darkness, a tall being wearing garish robes stepped forward. He smiled at the Hulk as he continued to clap his elegant, slim hands.

"That was masterful, absolutely masterful," he burbled enthusiastically. "Really. You are going to make quite the addition to my Contest of Champions. In fact, I think you might even be the Champion one of these days. Perhaps my most precious Champion."

Hulk snorted. "Who?" Hulk said curtly. Did the question come from him or Banner? He didn't know.

"Ah, yes, where are my manners?" the being said, as if in response. He had a blue streak that ran from his lip down to his chin. Placing his left hand on his chest, he said, "I'm the Grandmaster. And you are...."

"Leaving," said the Hulk, and he started to walk away from the Grandmaster. He didn't see a door at first, but there had to be one around somewhere.

"I wouldn't do that if I were you," the Grandmaster said. His tone wasn't at all threatening. In fact, it sounded full of concern.

The Hulk took one more step before his world filled with a white-hot pain he had felt once before, in the wasteland. It was as if the pain of every single transformation he had experienced, every time he'd gone from Banner to Hulk and back, had been compacted and distilled into this one moment. Hulk crumpled to the ground, writhing.

"See, I told you not to do that, and then that happened,"

the Grandmaster said. "You're wearing an Obedience Disc now, my friend. I wish it wasn't necessary, but, well, you can see how it is."

As the pain began to subside, the Hulk put one big green hand on the side of his neck. That must be what Scrapper had used to subdue him in the first place. In all the chaos that ensued after, he hadn't noticed anything attached to his body. Well, he certainly noticed the small, circular mechanical device attached to his neck now. *This is how they'll control us*, Banner thought from within.

Hulk didn't want to think.

Hulk wanted to smash.

He grabbed at the Obedience Disc, and received another terrible jolt of pain for his trouble.

"Oh, now, now, don't grab it," said the Grandmaster. "Don't ever grab it. That's going to be quite painful as well." He wasn't gloating at all. Rather, he actually seemed concerned for the Hulk's welfare. "Best to leave it alone and listen. I think we have a great deal to offer you, and you certainly have a great deal to offer us. Me, I mean. You seem to like smashing things, yes?"

That got the Hulk's attention. He looked up at the Grandmaster and cocked his head slightly.

"Ah, yes, I assumed so. Then you'll definitely like

it here. I can offer you almost unlimited opportunity to smash. In return, you fight before adoring crowds. I mean, they'll love you. What's not to love about you? You're big, you're green, you smash things. What do you say? Stay here and fight for me on the planet Sakaar, and be hailed as a true Champion."

Wait. What? What was going on here? Banner thought.

But the Hulk didn't want to think. He liked what he heard.

"Hulk stay ... for now."

CHAPTER 6

The fight continued for hours. Thor, encountering what had to be armies upon armies of Fire Demons, made his way across a scorched, perpetual battlefield. The clashes were serving their purpose, for Thor was certainly distracted from his disturbing visions.

The visions. Something he had glimpsed in those unsettling visions had brought Thor to this infernal place.

"Have at thee!" Thor shouted, his lungs burning as he drew in the scalding air of Muspelheim. Another wave of Fire Demons threw themselves upon the son of Odin. It seemed like he could keep at this all day, a thought that reminded Thor of his fellow Avenger, Captain America. That was something the Super-Soldier liked to say when things were at their most bleak and it seemed like he might lose the fight – "I could keep this up all day." Thor smiled as he continued to hurl Fire Demons away from him.

"Are you mad, Asgardian?" a Fire Demon screeched at Thor. "Even if you defeat us all, you have earned the wrath eternal of Surtur! He will pull the flesh from your bones while you writhe in agony!"

It hit Thor like a bolt of lightning from mighty Mjolnir.

Not the Fire Demon's threat. That did not concern the son of Odin. No, it was the name that the Fire Demon had mentioned that had awoken the memory within Thor.

Surtur.

The absolute ruler of Muspelheim.

In the midst of battle, Thor now remembered why he had come to Muspelheim. He remembered a figure he had glimpsed in his visions, someone ... something that sat at the centre of them.

Surtur.

Thor smiled once more, standing up straight, like a king.

"I would have a word with your master!" Thor called. "Tell Surtur I have come for him! Will he not face me? Or is your lord and master afraid of one Asgardian?" He wasn't sure if his boastful taunt could be heard above the din of Fire Demons and roaring flames of Muspelheim.

So he decided to get Surtur's attention.

Raising Mjolnir towards the heavens, Thor once more channelled the power of the storm itself, and called for nature to do his bidding. The sky rumbled with thunder, and lightning cascaded from the roiling clouds above. It struck the ground everywhere, or so it seemed. Fire Demons far and wide were racked with electricity. They flailed, unable to stop it, unable to do anything but succumb to the Asgardian's relentless assault.

Then the impossible happened. Something that had never before occurred in Muspelheim. Something Surtur himself could never have predicted.

It began to rain.

In the Realm of Fire.

A torrential downpour, summoned by Thor.

The driving rain hit the ground so hard that it stung even Thor's body. It pummelled the harsh terrain of Muspelheim unforgivingly. Great clouds of steam formed, making it almost impossible for Thor to see his foes, or anything else, for that matter.

And then – the screams.

The screams of the Fire Demons, experiencing an agony they had never felt before. The agony of endless rain eating away at their fiery bodies.

Once more, Thor cried out, "Tell Surtur I have come for him!"

CHAPTER 7

"You're next for processing. Follow me."

Hulk heard the voice and walked through the dimly lit hallway into a large room. On every wall, as far as he could see, were weapons. Armour. All kinds, all shapes, all sizes. There were axes and spears and hammers and scythes and bludgeons and truncheons and helmets and shields and on and on. Some looked familiar to Hulk, very much like Earth armaments. Others were completely alien to him – in fact, they probably were alien. He thought he recognized some weapons that the Chitauri had used in their attempted invasion of New York.

What was this place?

As if in answer, a hefty alien wearing a leather apron greeted the jade giant. He looked up at the Hulk.

He looked down at the Hulk. He did it again.

Wash, rinse, repeat.

"I am here to arm you for your upcoming match," said the alien in the leather apron.

Hulk grunted.

"Something tells me that you don't need a weapon."

Hulk shook his head in agreement. "Hulk is weapon."

"I'm sure. Still, take this," the alien in the leather apron said, holding out a huge battle-axe. The axe had two blades—on one side, a small one that ended in a sharp point. On the other, a much larger blade with jagged teeth. The alien tried to shove it into the Hulk's hands.

The green goliath made no effort to raise his hands and take the axe.

"Hulk is weapon," he repeated.

The alien all but rolled his eyes and pressed a button on the device he was carrying.

For the third time that day, Hulk learned what it meant to wear an Obedience Disc. If he was the strongest one there was, then this was the worst pain there was.

The Obedience Disc crackled as the Hulk roared in agony. As soon as it started, it stopped.

"Take this," the alien said, motioning to the battle-axe in his hands.

The Hulk drew in a deep breath, and picked up the axe. He sneered at the alien, grunting.

Stay calm, Banner thought from inside the Hulk.

Don't want to stay calm, Hulk thought. *Want to smash*.

"I've seen that look before, a hundred times," said a voice as the Hulk heard someone enter the room. "A thousand times. Probably more than that. You want to hit him. Save it. Use it in the battle to come."

The Hulk grunted as he saw a woman walking towards him. A woman with tattooed arms, wearing armour.

Angry Girl. The one they called Scrapper.

"The Grandmaster has a lot of faith in you," she said. "He's betting that you might become the new Champion."

The Hulk stared at Scrapper. "Why Angry Girl here?" he said, turning his attention back to the battle-axe he didn't want but was being forced to take.

Scrapper smiled at the moniker. "I also think you have the makings of a Champion," she said. "I thought you should know that before you entered the arena."

With that, the woman turned round and left.

CHAPTER 8

As swiftly as Thor had brought the driving, punishing rains to Muspelheim, he banished them. By his command, and through Mjolnir's will, the rains ceased. The screams of the Fire Demons subsided.

For a brief moment, no Fire Demon dared attack the son of Odin. Not when they realized what power he wielded, and could wield again, if he so chose.

So he said, for the last time, quite calmly, "Surtur. Take me to him."

The Fire Demons grew silent, wary of the Asgardian, and stared at him suspiciously. They must have realized that they were playing a zero-sum game with Thor.

They must be communicating with their master, he thought, satisfied.

Suddenly, Thor was struck with yet another terrible vision. He closed his eyes against the intruding images, not wanting to show weakness in front of the Fire Demons. Thor knew in the core of his being that the visions were an omen, a herald of things to come. He would know more of this vision. For somehow – and it had been blocked from his mind until today – he now realized who was sitting at the centre of his visions.

Surtur.

But why? What was the lord of this fiery realm doing in these awful visions that plagued him so?

Thor breathed out in relief as, slowly, the vision subsided, leaving him shaken but upright. He didn't know what these visions meant. But he would have answers. And only Surtur could provide them.

What happened next was completely predictable and yet wholly unexpected.

The predictable: the Fire Demons had, in fact, communed with Surtur – or rather, Surtur had communed with the Fire Demons – and Surtur had demanded that the son of Odin be brought before him.

Of course, Thor knew that he would not be received as

a "special envoy" from Asgard, afforded all the comforts of a diplomat. Not after the way he had entered Muspelheim. Not after the battles and vanquished Fire Demons. Not after the driving rain. No, the only way he would see Surtur would be as a prisoner.

The wholly unexpected: this was exactly what Thor wished.

"You belong to Surtur now," crackled a Fire Demon, who beckoned Thor forward. "He will grant you an audience. In turn, you shall be his prisoner until you die."

Thor nodded. "I shall come along quietly, then. Do you have handcuffs, or ...?" He extended both arms, offering up his wrists to the Fire Demons as if the Demons were the police and he a common thief. They looked at Thor, then at each other, not understanding. Handcuffs were probably not exactly standard issue in Muspelheim, Thor thought to himself, enjoying his joke.

"The hammer," said a Fire Demon, gesturing at Mjolnir. "Surrender the hammer."

"Yes, can't have an armed man going to see Surtur." Thor kneeled down and placed Mjolnir on the ground. "I'll see you soon," he said to the enchanted mallet, giving it a tender pat as one would a treasured pet.

As Thor began to trail after the Fire Demons towards

Surtur – and his fate – he heard a commotion behind him that caused him to look over his shoulder. A number of Fire Demons had raced over to Mjolnir and were each trying in turn to lift the mallet. They struggled and pulled and tugged and failed in their efforts.

For only one who was truly worthy could lift Mjolnir.

It was just as Thor wanted.

As he traversed the searing soil, surrounded by silent, sparking Fire Demons on all sides, Thor had a good deal of time to think. When he wasn't dwelling on Surtur and the vision, he thought about his life, what he had been doing with it. Ever since he had arrived on Midgard and made friends on that world, he had been splitting his time between being an Avenger and being heir to the Asgardian throne and protector of the Nine Realms. Sometimes he was the dutiful son of Odin, helping his fellow Asgardians through their trials and tribulations. His adopted brother, Loki, saw to it that there were troubles aplenty. Loki, the God of Mischief. The trickster. Master of lies and deceit. How many problems had he caused for Thor, his family and his friends?

Loki had been the catalyst that brought the Avengers

together in the first place, Thor remembered.

The Avengers. More and more, Thor had been spending his time on Earth with the Avengers. Their problems became his problems. Their battles, his battles. Their victories, his victories.

The team ... their friendship ... meant more to him than they could possibly know.

Still....

Thor felt something else. It wasn't a feeling he was used to, and it wasn't one he necessarily liked. The pangs of guilt. He felt guilty. Guilty for the time he'd spent away from Asgard and his brethren. As the rightful heir to the Asgardian throne, should he not have been by his father's side, instead of fighting beside the people of Midgard? What would Odin think? Were Thor's increasingly frequent absences the cause of the terrible visions?

He wiped the sweat from his brow and continued the long march to see Surtur. Thor swore he would have his answers yet.

CHAPTER 9

The Hulk could hardly believe what he saw.

There he was, stranded on an alien world – Sakaar – standing in the middle of an enormous arena. Bigger than any stadium he had ever seen on Earth. As he turned his head and looked around, he saw an endless sea of beings sitting in rows upon rows of seats. There were some humans scattered among the crowd (at least, beings who appeared to be human), but mostly he saw faces that clearly belonged to beings from the furthest reaches of space. And all these beings were cheering. They were hungry. Hungry for entertainment.

And in the middle of it all stood the Incredible Hulk.

Raising his head skyward, the Hulk saw great starships that appeared to hover directly above the arena. Above that, of course, were the ubiquitous wormholes: brilliant, swirling, ejecting junk in the distant horizon.

And then there was the twenty-metre-tall alien clad in elegant robes, standing in front of him. This confused the Hulk. How had the Grandmaster become so huge? From inside, Banner realized this must be a projection of some kind – a way for the Grandmaster to communicate to the huge crowd and enforce his will.

The Hulk just wondered why he was so big.

"Friends!" called the Grandmaster, and the crowds cheered even louder. Their voices were as one, roaring in Hulk's ears.

"We have a new arrival to our Contest of Champions! The Hulk ... of Earth!"

Again, the crowds roared.

What is this? Banner thought from inside the Hulk.

"Will he be able to defeat ..." The Grandmaster paused for dramatic effect before continuing. "... our Champion from Chitauri?"

That's when the Hulk saw it. A burly, ripped, cyborg-like creature holding two long staves. It was easily the same size as the Hulk. Striding into the arena, the creature swung the staves in wide circles. It was putting on a show for the crowd, and they loved it. The cheers grew louder.

Hulk wasn't distracted by the cheers. He stared at his opponent.

Now Hulk really wanted to smash.

An encouraging roar rose up from the crowd as the Chitauri landed yet another blow against the Hulk.

Hulk gritted his teeth and popped up again from the ground where he'd fallen. The noise that came from the crowd would have deafened an ordinary human. But the Hulk was not an ordinary human. His gamma-irradiated body was testament to that. The green goliath could tell who the people were cheering for, and it wasn't him. The Chitauri alien that he now faced must have been a favourite, for the crowd went wild every time he struck the Hulk with one of his staves.

Which, surprisingly, was happening more often than the Hulk would have liked.

Whenever the Chitauri landed even a glancing blow, the staves sparked and sent jolts of pure agony through the Hulk's nervous system. It felt like the Obedience Disc, only slightly less painful.

Hulk hated the staves.

He hated the Chitauri even more.

If he could just get the staves away from the Chitauri, then Hulk would smash and that would be the end of that.

WHAM! The Chitauri hit the Hulk right in his solar plexus, knocking the jade giant on to his knees yet again. The crowd went wild.

The Hulk struggled to his feet and faced his foe once more.

Gotta be smart about this, thought Banner.

Gotta smash, thought the Hulk.

Hulk roared, a sound that, for a split second, rose above the din of the crowd and shocked the raucous audience into momentary silence. Then he brandished his battle-axe in both hands. What he did next was unexpected. He snapped the axe in two and flung the pieces away. The axe was getting him nowhere. He didn't like using it when he could use his fists instead.

The Chitauri warrior saw this as an opening. He raced towards the Hulk, twirling a stave in each hand. As he advanced, the Hulk clapped his massive hands together. The resulting force caught the unsuspecting Chitauri warrior off guard and threw him backwards. Before he knew what was happening, the Chitauri was flat on his back in the arena, with the Hulk towering over him. The Hulk was on him. He grabbed the two staves and threw them into the air.

They didn't come down.

At least, not anywhere near the arena.

Then the Hulk picked up the Chitauri warrior, and threw him into the air.

He didn't come down, either.

Hulk whirled around, looking at the crowd, grunting. The masses remained silent.

"Fantastic," came a booming voice that filled the arena. "Fantastic! The victor is ... the Hulk of Earth!"

Then the cheering started once more. Slowly at first. Then the sound grew and grew as people from all over the stadium rose to their feet, applauding their new fighting hero.

The Hulk realized that the crowds were cheering for him.

Not for Banner.

For Hulk.

The man-monster felt something inside, something he had never felt before. He felt, at last, like he belonged.

The Hulk smiled.

He was finally home.

EPILOGUE

Before.

Before Ultron.

Before Sakaar, before Muspelheim.

Before the Hulk's self-imposed exile.

It was night, and the Avengers had gathered at Stark Tower. There was no official business this evening, no world that needed saving. It was just a chance to share a meal and each other's company. As the others gathered around, Thor found himself looking out of a window that loomed large over the city of New York.

"It's not Asgard, but it's still impressive, right?"

Thor turned his head to see Bruce Banner standing next to him. The scientist smiled warmly, and Thor returned it.

"Very much so. It's just as beautiful, in its own way,"

Thor replied. He turned back to the window, and then looked at Banner once more. "You know, Banner, there is something I've been wanting to ask you since the Battle of New York."

Banner took a long pull from the bottle of water he had in his hand. "What's on your mind?"

"I'm not sure what you recall from your time as the Hulk. We were fighting the Chitauri, you and I. Riding atop the back of a great flying beast."

Banner looked upwards, as if searching his memory. "Vaguely...."

"Do you recall us smashing through the wall of Grand Central Station?" Thor asked.

Banner continued to look upwards. "Vaguely...."

"And do you remember our victory over the creature?"

Banner shook his head from side to side. "To be honest, my memory gets a little fuzzy where the Hulk's concerned."

Thor sighed. "Well, then. There's no point in asking my next question."

Banner gave Thor a serious look. "No, ask. Come on, before everyone gets here and this party goes full-on Stark."

"Very well. It's just I assume, based on your vague

recollections, that you have no memory of punching me clear across the station."

Banner shook his head again. "No," he said. "No, I remember that like it just happened. *WHAM!* You went flying." The scientist laughed a little to himself.

Thor was incredulous. "How is it that you can remember that, but you have only the vaguest recall of everything else?"

The scientist shrugged. "Maybe I only remember the good times."

Banner smiled at Thor, and the two men laughed and clinked their glasses.

LET THE
BATTLE BEGIN

CHAPTER 1

First, there was the heat. Of that much, he could be sure. It radiated everywhere, the sound of flames crackling, the smell of sulphur and smoke lingering in the air with every breath.

His breath. That came second. Thor drew several big breaths in as he tried to get his bearings. Every exhale bounced back on to his face quickly, letting him know he was in a confined space. A coffin?

Third were the chains. He was bound head to toe in heavy iron chains. They held him tightly, fastened at his feet. He was shackled, hanging upside down, and a wooden box the size the dead were buried in was all that was separating him from an unknown, raging fire.

In short? Thor had definitely had better days.

He flexed slightly, testing the strength of his bonds. They didn't give. Thor inhaled the hot air into his lungs and flexed with all of his Asgardian might. His muscles strained. Suddenly, he felt the chains begin to bend until, with a sharp *CRACK* they flew off him. With a loud boom, the exploding chains blew open the box, sending pieces of wood splintering in all directions. Thor flipped in mid-air and landed on the ground below. He was free ... or so he thought. Looking around, he realized he had only traded one small cell for a much larger one.

Brushing back his long, tousled blond hair that had become as unruly as his beard of late, Thor surveyed his surroundings. He was in a large cavern. Dark stalactites and stalagmites grew from the ground and ceiling. The walls, though dark in colour, seemed to dance. Thor narrowed his gaze and peered closely at the shapes moving across the surfaces and realized there was fire inside the walls themselves.

With that, Thor realized where he was: Muspelheim.

Turning his attention to the centre of the room, his suspicions were confirmed. A large throne rose from the ground. It was dark and foreboding. And it was far too large for the skeletal figure that lay slumped upon its seat. Thor, his armour worn, beard grizzled and cape slightly torn, wondered how much better he looked than the worn being before him.

"Demon!" Thor cried out. "Reveal yourself. I have freed myself, now I seek audience with my captor."

His words echoed through the chamber hall. The skeleton looked on at him with its empty eye sockets. No reply.

After a few moments, however, he began to hear the sound of rushing wind. The echo became mocking laughter as it rushed towards the skeleton on the throne. Slowly, fire began to glow from within its bones. Within moments there was a fiery aura emanating around the entire creature as the skeleton began to sit upright in its throne.

"The Son of Odin wishes to see me?" the voice boomed from the skeleton.

"Well, that is certainly an improvement," Thor noted, a wry smile crossing his face.

"You may have escaped your prison, but you shall never escape Muspelheim alive." The skeleton seemed to laugh at Thor.

"Even after being held captive and strung upside down, I believe I can handle a bag of bones such as yourself," Thor replied.

Just then, from the walls, the ceiling, the floor, the entire cave lit up as the skeleton caught fire and began to grow. It expanded in size, filling the throne and transforming into a deadly creature of pure flame. It leaned forward and laughed again at Thor, its maw gaping wide open with evil mirth.

Thor gazed upon his captor, recognizing his fire-filled countenance where he hadn't before. "Surtur. At last. This look suits you much better, I must say."

"You dare mock me in my own chambers?" Flames shot out in all directions at Surtur's wrath. Surtur rose from his throne, a flaming giant, towering above Thor. "I was to bring you to Odin when I returned to Asgard and show him how far his son has fallen. I had hoped to return you alive, but no matter. With or without you, I shall retrieve the Eternal Flames stolen from me by Odin centuries ago."

"I haven't been back to Asgard in some time, but I doubt my father would strike such a deal. Those Flames are locked deep away for the protection of the Nine Realms." Thor began to smile.

"I see no reason for you to smile, Son of Odin," Surtur growled. "You have no hope of escape."

A slight pounding began to thud, coming closer and closer. Looking around, Surtur's eyes widened. "What is that sound?"

Thor's smile expanded into a wide grin, and he held out his arm. "Hope."

With that, the ground below him exploded and his trusted hammer, Mjolnir, flew into his outstretched hand.

"You wish to return to Asgard, demon? I shall bring you myself." Thor crouched, holding his hammer close to his side, about to leap. With a mighty flex of his powerful legs, he launched himself directly at Surtur. "No need for all of you to come, though. Just your skull!"

With a swift movement, Thor swung Mjolnir and connected with Surtur's jaw in a powerful uppercut, knocking the demon back and off his feet. Thor landed deftly on the ground, readying himself for another attack. Surtur roared in shock and pain. Flames began to grow around him as he summoned the fire. With a gesture of one bony flame-encased hand, the wall of fire went flying directly at Thor.

Thor began to spin Mjolnir, faster and faster, whipping up a windstorm. The wind created a protective dome around him and the flames from Surtur's attack passed by him. The wind extinguished another attack as Surtur hurled a fireball at Thor. The Fire Demon became more and more enraged.

Without warning, Thor ran towards the giant Fire Lord and, at the very last second, slid between his legs. Swinging his arm, he used Mjolnir to knock Surtur's knees out from under him, causing the villain to fall to the ground with a scream.

Thor stood above him, holding Mjolnir.

"The next time you wish to see Asgard, do not use the God of Thunder as your bargaining chip. Even flames can burn, Surtur." With that, he lifted Mjolnir high and the air around him began to crackle. Then, from above, came a magnificent bolt of lightning, striking Surtur in the chest as it surrounded Thor's foe. Surtur screamed in agony.

Thor stood above the Fire Lord's head, ready to deliver the final blow, when something caught his attention in the walls. It was one pair of eyes, and then another, and another. Dozens of eyes began to flicker. The flames that had seemed earlier to dance in the walls suddenly gained form. Humanoid Fire Demons appeared and began to spill from the walls in droves! A screeching noise caused Thor to look up and he saw the demons descending from the ceiling as well. He felt the burning touch as more grew from the floor, grabbing at his legs.

Thor's shock wore off quickly as he turned to face his foes, which greatly outnumbered him. "Your father has fallen, yet the minions come forth to try and finish what he could not? Sorry, but I am done playing games here."

Looking up, Thor cried to the heavens. "Heimdall! The Bifrost, please," he called, expecting the usual beam of rainbow energy to appear and transport him on to the bridge that allowed passage out of and into Asgard. But there was nothing.

Thor cried out again to his friend on Asgard who controlled the bridge. "Heimdall? Heimdall?!"

The demons rushed at Thor and quickly engulfed him, piling upon him two storeys high. They cackled in their apparent victory. Thor's echoes pleading for the Bifrost rang plaintively through the halls of Surtur's lair, unanswered.

CHAPTER 2

The rainbow bridge of the Bifrost, which looked out on to almost all of creation itself, linking each of the Nine Realms, gleamed brightly with cosmic energy. The golden-gilded, domed observatory where it originated from rose out of a platform at the edge of Asgard. The bridge itself spilled forth from a giant opening, usually controlled by Heimdall, the all-seeing, who normally operated it with a powerful sword in the centre of the dome.

But at the moment, the sword that controlled the Bifrost was missing. And so was Heimdall.

A glow from the centre of the controls to the Bifrost, which Heimdall would have activated to take those in need back to Asgard via the Bifrost's magical properties, pulsed. And pulsed. And pulsed.

"This?" said a voice from just outside the dome. "This is only one of the most powerful items in all the realms. And Odin has entrusted me with it."

The voice did not belong to the mighty Heimdall, who never left his post. Instead, a balding man with a slight sneer that was meant to be a smile was showing off to two Asgardian women. "'Skurge,' Odin said to me. 'You are far more suited to guard the entrance to Asgard than that traitor Heimdall'," the man bragged. "That's when he gave me this sword."

"You must be a brave man to be given such a great responsibility," one of the Asgardian women said. His attempts to impress them were clearly working, Skurge thought, quite pleased with himself.

"Oh, the battles I've seen. They would chill your blood. The beasts on Vanaheim had four heads each. Yet I stood my ground and fought them back. I believe that's why he rewarded me." Skurge smiled. "Come, let me show you a view like you've never seen before."

With that, Skurge and the two women exited the dome, none of them noticing the beacon pulsing insistently, someone clearly calling on the Bifrost for assistance.

CHAPTER 2

In Muspelheim, a mound of Fire Demons continued to pile on to the spot where Thor once stood. Surtur began to recover from the bolt of lightning to his chest and rose from the ground, emitting a shriek of glee. His laughter was cut short, though, as suddenly the outer ring of Fire Demons were flung backwards off the pile, shaken by a rumbling. Without warning, Mjolnir burst forth from the top of the mound, sending Fire Demons flying in a volcanic fashion.

The hammer flew around the room, ricocheting off the walls and ceiling, knocking back Fire Demons left and right. Surtur watched in horror as victory was seemingly once again snatched away from him. He ducked as the hammer flew back towards where the Fire Demons had overpowered Thor, only to see the God of Thunder himself standing there, no worse for wear, catching Mjolnir in one outstretched hand as it returned to its owner.

"I believe my visit to your realm has come to an end, Surtur. I prefer milder climes." Swinging Mjolnir, Thor flew up and burst through the top of the cavern.

Thor landed heavily on the ground and called out to Heimdall once more for the Bifrost. He was perplexed. Never had his request been denied; his friend was always at the ready to send him the means needed to return

to Asgard. His thoughts were interrupted by a rumbling sound. Perhaps it was the Bifrost, opening to him at last? Turning, he saw the source of the noise, and his heart sank.

Where he'd hoped a beam of energy would alight from above and envelop him to take him home, stood a mighty fire dragon, easily 30 metres long, and full of rage. The beast bellowed and flames shot forth. Thor flew out of the way to dodge the attack and, directing Mjolnir towards the sky, flew upwards to escape the beast's wrath. But the dragon took to the skies to follow the hero. Thor dodged burst after burst of flames shot forth from the dragon's mouth.

Swiftly, Thor spun in the air and charged the dragon. Catching it off-guard, he delivered a blow that knocked the dragon backwards. As the dragon fell, Thor continued to pummel it as it crashed to the ground. At last, back on Muspelheim's surface and standing above it, Thor held Mjolnir over the defeated creature's head.

"Only those worthy may lift the mighty hammer Mjolnir, foul demon-spawn." He dropped the hammer on the dragon's head. Struggling, the dragon could not raise his head from under Mjolnir. "Clearly, you are not worthy."

Thor turned his attentions to the heavens once more.

THOR

When an ancient evil is released from its cursed imprisonment and seeks revenge, Thor is thrown into a whirlwind of chaos.

Suddenly, Thor finds himself torn from his familiar surroundings and stripped of his powers. His only hope is to summon the warrior within and fight his way back to Asgard to save his people – and the universe.

HULK

Hulk has been missing since the Avengers' last adventure.
His whereabouts are finally discovered when Thor stumbles
upon him in an unlikely location – a cosmic battle arena
halfway across the galaxy.

Basking in the glory of being a battle Champion, Hulk
is reluctant to return to his former life. But when a dangerous
threat against the universe looms he must decide where his
strength is needed most.

HELA

Hela is a creature from the prehistoric and sinister era of the universe, and her power is unlike anything else in the Nine Realms.

Armed with the ability to unleash unlimited weapons, Hela seeks vengeance against those who imprisoned her eons ago. She wants to bring a new age of cold brutality to Asgard and the universe.

LOKI

Loki is up to his old tricks again ... he has disguised himself as his father, Odin, and assumed control over Asgard. He is revelling in finally being king.

However, when dangers from Odin's past start to surface, Loki must use his quick wit and skill with a blade to battle for survival in the fight of his life.

VALKYRIE

After a mysterious tragedy left Valkyrie's life in tatters, she disappeared to a corner of the universe where she could forget her past. She now works as a fierce galactic scavenger.

But with the universe in danger, Valkyrie must put her past behind her and join forces with Thor and Hulk to save Asgard in its darkest hour.

THE GRANDMASTER

The Grandmaster is the exuberant and dangerous ruler of a distant planet built on chaos and indulgence.

He controls the Contest of Champions – the gladiatorial competition in which Thor, Hulk and other powerful beings from throughout the universe battle in spectacular and deadly combat.

HEIMDALL

Heimdall guards the Bifrost Bridge, the gateway into Asgard. He is one of Asgard's fiercest warriors, armed with an incredible broadsword and the ability to see anywhere in the universe at any given moment.

When Hela and her sinister plans threaten the world Heimdall has sworn to protect, he must step up and defend its people.

SKURGE

Skurge has an obsession with weapons and equipment from other worlds. The Asgardian soldier has collected an arsenal of strange and powerful weapons from across the Nine Realms.

Now, in Asgard's time of need, Skurge must use his amazing armoury to ensure its survival.

"Heimdall! The Bifrost, please. I am quite finished here."
He waited a moment, but nothing. His attention away
from the dragon, he didn't notice the beast slowly begin
to swish its deadly tail.

"That was beautiful," marvelled one of the Asgardian
women as they re-entered the dome of the Bifrost.

"Oh," chuckled Skurge, "That was nothing. I have an
even better view for you if you ladies wish to join me –"

The other woman pointed at the pulsing from the
Bifrost controls. "Is that normal?"

Skurge paled. "Uhhhhh, of course. Yes. You are ..."
he frantically searched for the sword that controlled the
Bifrost, which he had carelessly tossed into a corner after
he'd finished displaying it to the women. "... are about
to see.... Ah! There it is!" He grabbed the sword and ran to
the controls. "Would you like to see the Bifrost in action?"
His face contorted into his version of a smile as he inserted
the sword and turned it. The Bifrost's centre began to spin
as its immense energy powered up.

WHOOF! Thor was knocked off his feet by the dragon's

tail. The beast had been inching ever closer as Thor waited for the Bifrost and Heimdall. Suddenly, his face was mouth level with the dragon. He saw flames begin to form. Grabbing Mjolnir, Thor leaped from the ground seconds before being burned to a crisp and took to the skies once more.

The dragon, now freed from the hammer's weight, followed in pursuit. Ahead, Thor at last spotted the familiar swirling of Bifrost energy. It was about time! He sped up, the dragon fast on his heels. As the opening cleared, Thor zoomed through it. The dragon's head entered the Bifrost a second later.

"Are you ready to witness something none but the luckiest on Asgard has ever seen?" Skurge was almost sweating with excitement and the chance to brag before two of the most beautiful Asgardians he had ever entertained. This Keeper of the Bifrost thing certainly had its perks.

The Bifrost opened and immediately Thor came flying through!

"Close it! The Bifrost! Now!" Thor bellowed, sliding to a halt in the centre of the dome. As Skurge twisted the control, the head of the flame dragon entered through the

Bifrost ... and was quickly severed from his body by the gate's closing. The decapitated head slid across the floor of the dome and landed at the feet of the two women, who screamed and promptly fled.

Thor could barely contain his rage as he turned on this stranger before him. Standing at full height, covered in dragon's blood and singed from his fight with the Fire Demons, he strode towards Skurge. "Who are you and where is Heimdall?"

Skurge tried to stand tall, but the sight before him made his spine and legs not want to cooperate. He cleared his throat, attempting to speak with some authority. "I – I am Skurge, Keeper of ... of the Bifrost."

"Some 'keeeper' you are. Did you not hear my many calls?" Thor was nearly toe-to-toe with the Asgardian, who was still attempting to remain brave.

"I was ... attending to other business."

"So I saw." Thor looked around. "You claim to be the keeper; where is Heimdall?"

Skurge scoffed before he could stop himself. "That traitor? Banished."

"Traitor? Heimdall? Never! Who laid such claims?" Thor was shocked.

Skurge smiled. This was the one part he liked to say

to anyone who would listen. "Why, by Odin himself. And it was Odin who named me Keeper of the Bifrost, as reward for my service and –"

"Odin? I think not." Thor interrupted. He turned and flew off in the direction of the palace.

Skurge ran after Thor, but slipped in a puddle of dragon slime. "Wait! Only I can announce you to Odin! 'Tis his orders!" Covered in muck, Skurge gave up trying to run after Thor, who was by then but a small dot on the horizon of Asgard.

Skurge groaned. He hoped he wouldn't lose his job because of this.

CHRPTER 3

"And so Loki, ever clever, was able to outwit the Dark Elf Malekith and save all of Asgard, though it meant sacrificing his life for his home, his father and all the Nine Realms. The end."

A chorus of clapping rose from the considerable crowd grouped around the stage. An actor was narrating a play being performed in the middle of a grand terrace to an audience filled with rapt Asgardians. At the head of the open-aired, makeshift theatre, seated upon a massive throne, was Odin, lounging to one side as he drank a goblet of wine.

"And destroyed the Aether, ending the Convergence. We mustn't forget that detail, mustn't we?" Odin directed from the throne.

The narrator nodded eagerly but, before he could revise the ending, a murmur rose from the crowd and grew in scale until the audience was positively atwitter. Odin turned, annoyed at the disturbance, and his heart sank.

Heading straight towards him was Thor. His gaze was trained on Odin as he strode through the parting crowd, all of whom were murmuring about the God of Thunder's return ... and his appearance.

"Father, I would have words with thee." Thor addressed Odin.

"Thor! Um, son!" Odin sat up straight suddenly, composing himself. "What an ... unexpected honour to have you return. You've just missed the most marvellous play about the life of your poor, fallen adoptive brother, Loki."

"It seems I have missed much," Thor returned pointedly, glowering at Odin.

"You're right. We should amend the ending to include Thor's role in the Great Battle," Odin directed to the royal scribe who was making notes on the play. He turned back to Thor. "Would you like to see the revisions, my son?"

"I heard enough already, thank you, Father." Thor began to approach the throne. Odin waved his hands and members of the Einherjar, his Royal Knights, escorted the citizens out of the terrace, allowing privacy between the two.

"It has been far too long since I have seen you, son."

"And I, you, it appears," Thor said.

"I must say, are you unwell? Because you look rather unlike yourself." Odin waved his hand at Thor's haggard, dragon-blood-soaked appearance.

Thor gave a wry smile. "Funny, I was going to say the same about you, 'Father'."

Odin shifted uncomfortably in his seat for a moment before suddenly standing and began to make his way out of the terrace. "Please, clean up and join me for, ah, supper. Wouldn't that be grand?"

Thor leaped and landed in front of Odin, blocking his path to the door. "You know my favourite thing about travels? The return home. It's like Mjolnir. No matter how far I throw it, it shall always return to my hand, even if something is in the way." Thor lifted Mjolnir high in his hand as though to throw it straight through Odin.

"Now wait there, just a moment, son —"

Thor began to swing Mjolnir around his head, whipping it into a faster and faster frenzy until the hammer was poised for release.

"All right, all right!" Odin cried out. There was a tense

beat and then "Odin" began to fade. The illusion gone, in his place stood Loki!

Thor shook his head in disbelief. "I wanted to be wrong about you, brother. How did you escape Death?"

"By evading its grasp in the first place, of course." Loki sneered at his adopted brother.

"Only you would make a mockery of your own sacrifice. I believed you'd changed, Loki. I believed you to be good and decent in the end." Thor was genuinely upset by uncovering this latest deceit in his brother's endless list of mischief and troubles.

"And I believed in unicorns and chocolate fountains, but some things are impossible, aren't they? Now, can we skip the sanctimonious lecture about how I fooled you yet again and get to the point I know you're dying to make, so you can go and shower at the very least?" Loki turned up his nose in disgust to emphasize his point.

"I nearly died thanks to your treachery and that buffoon you placed at the helm of the Bifrost. Where is Heimdall?"

Loki shrugged. "Wherever those who their king declares traitors and relieves them of duty go, I suppose."

"And where is Father?" Thor asked through gritted teeth.

"That is the question, isn't it?" Loki mused, smiling.

Thor balled his Mjolnir-free hand into a fist. "Now is not the time for tricks, Loki. I have felt something. Something dark coming, and we need Father."

"Do we really, though? I've managed quite well while you've been gone and he's been ... off." Loki seemed quite pleased with himself as a ruler.

"Take me to him now or I shall have Mjolnir meet the back of your head," Thor said, growling.

"That is one incentive, I suppose. But I assure you, there's nothing to fear. Asgard is as safe as it ever has been."

Thor's face darkened. "We must find Father to ensure that."

At the entrance to the Bifrost, Thor and Loki stood ready for the portal to be opened and transport them to wherever Loki was hiding Odin.

Loki moved towards Skurge and hissed, "I gave you one job! Keep my brother away."

Skurge shook visibly. "I'm sorry, Your Highness. But there was...." He looked over his shoulder at the decapitated dragon head in the corner of the observatory.

Loki turned to Thor. "Bringing home souvenirs now, brother?"

"I'm thinking of collecting heads and having them mounted on my wall. Care to join my newest trophy?" Thor retorted.

"My, my, such hostility. Asgard was certainly much more peaceful when I was in charge." Loki loved needling his brother and revelled in the annoyance it caused. Thor, however, merely waved off his heckling today, focused on other, more important matters.

"You, Skurp," he called out.

"It's Skurge, actually," the Asgardian replied.

"There is something not right among the universe and I fear it is heading towards Asgard. While we are gone, entertain yourself by performing the task at hand, rather than with wine and women." Thor was clearly not pleased that Heimdall was missing. "I've brought back-up for you."

Thor nodded to the entrance of the Bifrost observatory dome. Standing there, nearly filling the doorway, were Volstagg and Fandral, Thor's most trusted friends in life and battle. Skurge's jaw dropped open. "Two of the Warriors Three? I fought with you at Vanaheim. Skurge. It's an honour." He walked towards the duo, hand outstretched. Volstagg pulled a mop from behind his back and placed it firmly in Skurge's hand.

Fandral looked at the humbled Skurge. "It is time to clean house, I believe." He nodded to the dragon's head.

Volstagg laughed. "And don't miss a spot. Fandral is very particular."

The Bifrost powered up and a swirling portal opened. "Time to go, brother. Unless you have any other duties to assign?" Loki stepped through.

Fandral looked to Thor. "Do not worry, Odinson. We will be here to ensure your safe return. Even if Volstagg has to sit on this cretin to do it."

"We fought together," Skurge muttered under his breath.

Thor grasped his friend's hand in thanks and, with a final warning glare in Skurge's direction, vanished into the Bifrost.

CHAPTER 4

A pair of rats was scampering over the remains of a carton of discarded rotting fruit when a pair of feet wearing three pairs of socks in place of shoes shuffled by, scaring them off. The alley was just off 37th Street in New York City's "Flower District", a name that conveyed far more beauty than what actually met the eye if one looked closely enough into the abandoned and darkened spaces between buildings. The littered alleys held rubbish bins full of fruit and vegetables that had been fresh the day before but gone bad in the afternoon heat. By morning, they were thrown out and left for the forgotten beggars and animals to fight it out as that day's meal.

The man who'd scared off the rats wore tattered street clothes and looked as though he hadn't bathed in days.

A torn cloth covered his right eye. He rummaged through the bin and found a bunch of bananas, still perfectly wrapped. It was his lucky day!

He was tucking the almost-fresh produce into one of his many layers when a blinding light struck the dawn glow of the alley. When his eye adjusted, he saw two men approaching him, one of them wielding what appeared to be a large hammer. The man quickly glanced down and, spotting an abandoned piece of wood, picked it up and raised it like a sword.

"Stand and hold, foul ones. I was a great warrior in my day and I still know how to wield a weapon." He began to swing the piece of wood at the men, who stepped back, surprised.

Thor looked to his brother in confusion and spoke in a low tone. "New York? Why here, brother? And why show me this poor lost soul?"

They were dressed in regular Earth street wear, shirts and trousers, and Thor carried an umbrella. His hair was swept back into a ponytail. Loki's magic was projecting an illusion upon the duo.

Loki motioned for Thor to look again at their "attacker". Thor looked closely at the old man approaching them spouting gibberish. His long grey hair and appearance suggested he had lived on the streets for many years. The man stood tall for a moment, his hair brushed back, and it was then that Thor saw the telltale bandage covering one eye.

Before them stood no ordinary beggar: this was Odin, King of Asgard!

Thor's stomach dropped in sorrow and pity. "I shall never forgive you for this," he hissed at Loki as he approached the agitated man, his arms held out, trying to calm him.

"Back! Back, I say!" cried Odin.

"Father." Thor's voice cracked with emotion. "It is I, Thor." The dishevelled man stopped mid-swing. "Yes, Thor, your son. And this, the other I bring with me, is Loki."

"Thor. Loki." The man mumbled the words, a faint memory stirring as these names stirred something within him, but he couldn't quite grasp it.

"Yes, Father. And you are Odin, the King of Asgard and Protector of the Nine Realms," Thor continued, hoping to reach through the magic-induced amnesiac fog that clouded his father's mind.

"Asgard." This struck a chord with the man. "Asgard," he repeated. "Home?"

Thor nearly wept. "Yes, Father, Asgard is your home, and I've come to take you back and place you on the throne as its rightful ruler."

The man pushed back a strand of hair from his one good eye as he studied Thor. A spark of familiarity lit his clouded blue eye. He dropped the piece of wood and a tear formed.

"Thor? Loki? My sons." He held out his arms. "My sons!" His voice grew stronger as he embraced Thor. Loki turned away, partly in shame that his actions had put Odin in this situation, and partly in shock at being called "son" by Odin.

Thor held his father gently. The once-formidable ruler was so frail Thor could have carried him with one hand. How far his father had fallen under Loki's trickery! He wondered how long his father had suffered in these conditions.

"I'm sorry, Father, I never should have left. But come, we shall return, all three of us." Thor looked pointedly at Loki as though to say, don't even think about disappearing your way out of this one. Thor was helping to steady his father, who was gazing into his eyes.

As Thor was holding Odin, he felt the power of the All-Seeing One reach him even in Odin's weakened state.

"Tell me, my boy. What has you frightened so?"

"A feeling, Father. A darkness I cannot escape. I feel it has chased me, or I it, across the realms for months now. I went to Muspelheim thinking that the Fire Demon Surtur was the cause, but he knew nothing." Thor looked into his father's eye, hoping there would be some flicker of knowledge or recognition.

Odin pushed his son away and grabbed his head, crying out in pain. It seemed Thor had probed too deeply into long-buried memories and caused his father pain.

Thor turned on Loki, apoplectic with rage. "You cast him out, turned him homeless, made him forget who he was. Now he cannot remember even the stories he told us as warnings!" Thor's face reddened. "Tell me, Loki, was this necessary? How could even you do something so foul?"

Loki shrugged, trying to remain calm. "I did what I thought best. Maybe you wouldn't have done the same, but you never cared for the throne, anyway."

"Stories. The throne." Odin was struggling to right himself. Thor rushed to his father's side to help. "Hela." The word hung in the air like a shadow, chilling all three men in the alley to their bones.

"Hela? She is but a myth, Father. Stories told to frighten

children." Thor helped his father to his feet.

"Odinson." Thor looked at his father as Odin called him the name he felt he'd run from most of his adult life. "You are the Odinson. It is you who must return to Asgard, and quickly."

Thor shook his head. "No, Father. You are the rightful one to be seated on the throne. I am no king."

Odin grabbed him. "You must become one now, my son. This place, Asgard, all of the Nine Realms, need the Odinson to sit on the throne. Asgard needs its king, my child, and that is you."

Loki cleared his throat. "If I may, Asgard has flourished quite well under the reign of its current king. I don't see —"

Thor's steely look silenced Loki. Turning his gaze back on his father, he said, "This darkness I have felt and Hela, are they related?"

Odin put his hand to his head, as if the questions only caused him more pain. "I ... I can't...." He swatted at invisible foes that plagued his now-damaged mind. "The Odinson is needed on Asgard," he uttered at last. "If the darkness is coming, it will need protecting."

"Then we shall protect it together, the two of us, Thor and Odin," Thor said, lifting his umbrella. He struck it to the ground and suddenly he and Loki were dressed in their Asgardian clothes and armour. His father remained in tatters. "Come, Father, it is time to return you to your place."

He looked to Loki, who nodded.

"Skurge," Thor called out, "the Bifrost, if you will. Oh, and we have company," he added, looking at his father.

The energy from the Bifrost beamed down and covered the three of them and, in an instant, they were whisked out of the alley of New York City. The rats scurried from the shadows and began fighting over the bunch of fresh bananas Odin had left behind.

Along the Bifrost, Thor helped Odin walk across the Rainbow Bridge towards the domed observatory in the distance. Loki strode ahead of them, trying to not think of the many unpleasant punishments his brother and father must have in mind for him for when they returned to Asgard. So deep in thought was Loki that he failed to notice the subtle tremor that rocked the Bridge slightly.

Looking ahead at his brother, Thor wondered if perhaps he was seeing one of Loki's illusions. Could the Bifrost actually be shaking? Before he could ask, he saw black tendrils suddenly wrap themselves round the Bifrost before him. Looking back, more tendrils were quickly creeping up the other side of the Bridge, from where the trio had just landed.

"Brother!" Thor called out a warning, but Loki turned to him a moment too late. A part of the dark talon that seemed to be covering the Bridge and cutting them off from their destination swiftly struck Loki in the chest.

Loki felt himself lose his balance, but stood his ground against the black tendril. It struck again, this time aiming for his head. It found its mark and hit Loki square in his helmet, knocking him to the Bifrost's edge. Loki struggled to stay conscious, but everywhere he looked there seemed to be blackness.

Loki's fragile hold on the bridge slipped.

"No!" screamed Thor as he watched his brother fall off the edge of the Rainbow Bridge into the blackness of the cosmos below. He let go of his father briefly to rush ahead to where Loki had been. There was no sign of his brother.

The Bifrost shook again. With a sense of dread, Thor turned back, too late to act. The black tendrils had made their way up and now grasped Odin.

"Father!" Thor's cries seemed to be swallowed by the darkness that was covering the Bifrost.

"You are ... the Odinson...." His father's words hung in

the air as Odin was pulled from the Bifrost into the same darkness that had swallowed Loki up just moments ago.

With a roar, Thor hurled Mjolnir at the dark tendrils to drive them back and try to free his father. His trusted hammer cut through the blackness, revealing Odin was no longer there. Before it could return to Thor's hand, the dark tendrils closed around Mjolnir and it, too, vanished.

Thor stood alone on the Bifrost, weaponless, his father and brother both missing and darkness closing in fast upon him. He adopted a fighting stance, ready to attack his unseen foe with his fists if needed. "Come at me, then! Do your worst!"

As if answering his dare, the Bifrost shook with a great heave and Thor was knocked to its surface. Another quake shoved him towards the edge. The darkness that had been plaguing him for months seemed to form before him as one last tremor hurled him off the Bifrost.

He fell into nothingness, watching the darkness retreat from the Bifrost as his own darkness began to overtake him and he lost consciousness.

In the Bifrost observatory, Skurge, who had been left to clean alone after Fandral and Volstagg had activated the

Bifrost for Thor, paused in his mopping to look back at the Rainbow Bridge. To his surprise, there was no sign of anyone. He shrugged, and was about to turn away when he saw the most terrifyingly beautiful figure begin to appear from black tendrils at the far end of the Bifrost and advance towards him.

CHAPTER 5

Thor's eyes snapped open. He felt heavier than normal, the air thicker, dusty. He was not on the Bifrost, nor was he on Asgard, nor Earth. Even before looking around, Thor knew this place felt different to any world he'd ever been to.

Sitting up slowly, he took in his surroundings. The desolate landscape was littered, literally, with debris: broken pieces of ships, wheels, cracked weapons and other rubbish were piled everywhere. Thor glanced up and gasped. Where there should have been stars or a clear sky, instead there were hundreds of wormholes filling the sky above. Occasionally more debris would fall through one and crash to the ground. A broken space-ship came spilling out of a wormhole nearby and he watched as strange aliens hurriedly made their way in its direction. *Scavengers*, he thought.

Looking above him once again, Thor saw that the smaller wormholes were dwarfed by one massive wormhole, this one a deeper colour than the rest and which would occasionally light up as if electricity were coursing through it.

As he struggled to gain his bearings, a square ship hovered its way towards him. It reached nearer and suddenly broke apart into four smaller ships that descended and surrounded him. Before he could act, a pair of grotesque aliens exited each ship and aimed their weapons at him.

"Hold!" he cried, hands up. "I am not your foe."

Ignoring him, the aliens fired all at once. With a jolt, energy coursed through Thor as he was wrapped in electrical netting from all sides, knocking him again on to his back. He couldn't speak or move as the aliens closed in.

Something caught Thor's attention in the air above the aliens. A sleek ship, one well cared for and vastly different than the one the aliens had descended from, came to a halt, hovering above them. The top slid open and out jumped ... a woman! This was no ordinary woman. Her helmet revealed her face and she was smiling, apparently ready to enjoy the fight that was about to ensue.

Leaping down, she knocked out two aliens with one punch from her brass-knuckled fist. She turned and kicked away two more. The bracers that laced up her forearms began to entwine as though alive and cover her entire forearm and fist. Suddenly, an armoured fist shot from her hand and mimicked her gestures, grasping the last fleeing alien by the foot, picking him up and slamming him to the ground. The armour retracted to her fist and her bracers untwined themselves, going back to their original design on her arms.

The netting that held Thor still sent shock waves through his body, making it difficult for him to talk and impossible to move. Nevertheless, he smiled. He recognized what this woman was.

"You ... are ... Valkyrie." He smiled, speaking through the pain of the electricity coursing through his body. The Valkyrie were some of Asgard's fiercest warriors. He tried to reach out to his saviour. "I ... am ... Thor. Son of ... Odin."

"And I care because ...?" The woman clearly did not. She sneered down at him.

"Please ... for Asgard ... free me. Help me return. There ... is a darkness." Thor wondered why the woman was not moving to unbind him. He began to struggle against the netting, ignoring the pain that every movement brought on as he was shocked again and again.

"You're not on Asgard any more and there's plenty of darkness here, so get used to it," Valkyrie said as she spat out the word "Asgard".

Thor finally managed to free one arm. He reached out and nearly grabbed her leg in desperation. Valkyrie swiftly side-stepped him, and kicked his hand away with a solid roundhouse.

"You don't understand...." Thor tried again weakly.

"Oh, that's where you have it wrong. I understand perfectly." She aimed a small device at him and a disc shot out of it, embedding itself into Thor's chest. She took out a fob control, pushed a button, and sent a jolt through Thor.

The pain that ran through his body was unlike anything he'd ever felt. Thor's whole body stiffened, paralysed. Still, looking up at the woman, he muttered one last plea.

"For ... Asgard...." His voice was raspy as even his vocal cords began to stiffen along with the rest of him.

With a final swift kick to his head, Valkyrie knocked Thor out. She looked down at him. If she was surprised to see an Asgardian on this dismal planet, it didn't register on her face. Then again, she was not known for showing emotion. Getting the job done was her speciality.

She loaded Thor on to her ship and slid behind the controls. Taking out a communicator, she adjusted the dial and spoke into it. "Scrapper 142 reporting in. I have new cargo. Tell him to expect me soon. He'll want this one." She clicked off the communicator and looked back at the unconscious Thor.

"Welcome to Sakaar, Son of Odin." With that, she shifted the controls as her ship rose from the ground, banked away from the scavengers below, and headed to the city in the distance.

Back on Asgard, the Bifrost had barely finished breaking apart when the dark tendrils began to spill out of the observatory. They travelled to an overlook of the majestic land and swirled to form a single mass, taking on a humanoid figure. As Asgardians watched, the Einherjar marched out in force to face this mysterious threat. Within moments, the blackness had cleared away and in its place stood a woman.

It was clear this was no ordinary woman. Dressed in a leathery armour of black and green, with long black hair and an icy-cold look in her heavily shadowed eyes, the woman surveyed the realm before her. A hush fell over all of Asgard as it held its collective breath, waiting for her to speak.

When her voice sounded at last, it rang out clear and strong, full of authority in a tone that brooked no room for dissent. "I have returned, although most of you know me as a nightmare or fable. But I assure you, I am no tale. I am Hela, Queen of Hel, Ruler of the Underworld. Long ago, I was cast out of Asgard by Odin and his warriors, but my time to return has arrived. You are without a king on the throne. It is not the throne I seek, however. It is the end of Asgard itself. My name was once whispered as a possibility, a foretelling of events that could lead to the fall of your beloved realm."

Hela began descending the stairs from her overlook. The Einherjar readied their swords, spears and shields to protect the citizens of Asgard.

"I am no whisper. I am no possibility," Hela announced, her voice growing louder, like an approaching storm. She paused and every Asgardian felt she was looking directly into their fearful souls.

"I am an inevitability."

With that, she raised her arms and the entirety of the Einherjar were wiped out with one fell swoop of the dark tendrils. The people of Asgard inhaled a collective gasp of panic and began to run frantically, every which way, desperate to escape the evil that had descended upon their realm.

"Flee. Find shelter if you can," Hela's voice echoed through the land. "It matters not." With a tilt of her head, fires sprang up all around.

"I am the ruler of Death, and I assure this: Asgard is dead."

CHAPTER 6

With its vibrant colours and eclectic décor, the Grandmaster's chamber was nearly as unique as its owner.

Nearly.

Seated on a splendid couch, the Grandmaster, the ruler of all Sakaar, sipped a steaming beverage from a golden goblet.

"It looks like it's scalding hot, but it's actually quite refreshingly cool. That's the magic. Isn't it great?" he surveyed the room. His two handmaidens nodded in agreement obediently, while a sulking figure in the corner simply rolled her eyes in boredom. The rest of the room was filled with the highest of Sakaarian society. They were dressed in their culture's finest formal wear, creating a sea of glittering colours and jewels. They all nodded enthusiastically at the Grandmaster's proclamation of his drink's unique form and taste and began motioning to the servants, ordering these deceptive beverages for themselves. The Grandmaster sipped, smiling at the fact that he was, quite literally, a taste-maker. His delight with his beverage was interrupted, however, by a "zapping" noise, then a stifled cry of pain making its way towards his chamber.

"This ... ungg ... really isn't necessary, is it?" came a voice from the hallway as Valkyrie entered the chamber. Behind her, Thor struggled to follow as he was repeatedly electrocuted by the disc Valkyrie had attached to his chest.

The Grandmaster clapped twice and the room fell silent, all eyes on the brawny newcomer now felled to his knees at the centre of the opulent chamber. The Grandmaster looked closely at Thor. "A bit ragged, don't you think? But even diamonds start as coal, I guess." Turning his attention to Valkyrie, he asked, "What have you brought me?"

"A contender." Her curt reply was followed by her casual push of a button on her control, jolting Thor again, causing him to flex in response.

"Yes, yes. Real potential I see. A little make-over and the crowd will eat him up. Very nice, Scrapper 142. Wouldn't you agree, Topaz?"

The sulking figure in the corner gave only an icy stare

in response. Valkyrie smiled slightly at her rival. "Don't worry, I'm sure you'll find your own contender. That is, if you ever get up and actually search for once," she muttered under her breath, but loud enough for Topaz – and the rest of the room – to hear.

Grandmaster waved his hands benevolently, setting his beloved drink down delicately on its gilded saucer. "Ladies, please. This is a place of enjoyment and relaxation. No need for feuds. We leave that to the arena."

At the sound of the word, Thor looked to the Grandmaster. "What arena?"

"What arena?" Grandmaster chuckled. "Oh, Scrapper 142, this really is quite fresh meat."

"Which I expect to be paid for," she replied smartly, her hand outstretched.

"Yes, yes, your bounty." Grandmaster snapped his finger and a servant brought forth a bag of coins.

Valkyrie stared at the bag, then at Grandmaster. "Double for this one. Trust me. He's worth it."

Grandmaster sighed and snapped again and another servant brought a second bag. "What makes you so sure? I'm practically dying to know."

"Ask him yourself." Then Valkyrie turned and left the chamber, but not before giving Topaz a sly grin.

There was clearly an unspoken contest between them, and whatever prize contender Valkyrie had just dropped on Grandmaster's doorstep made her believe she'd just assumed the advantage.

"You paid her twice? I've brought you far better specimens. This one looks homeless, dragged from a gutter," Topaz protested. Grandmaster held up his hand to calm her.

"And I'm sure you will again, my dear. You know you're still my favourite. But if Scrapper 142 says there's something special about this one –"

"I can hear you. And I assure you, I'm far from a gutter-dweller." Thor rose to his full height. He walked towards the Grandmaster, but was suddenly zapped again and yelped in pain. Grandmaster held up a fob control identical to Valkyrie's.

"Just a precaution. I know the Obedience Discs can be a nuisance," he said. "But necessary in most cases. Although I haven't ever been very fond of the name. It was a working title while we were in the testing phase and no one seemed to put 'Find Better Name' on the agenda, so it stuck."

Thor struggled through the pain and stood up once again, gritting his teeth in determination, refusing to show any pain.

"Well, well. You are a contender, are you? Tell me, what's your story? Who are you, where do you come from?" Grandmaster sat back, genuine interest clearly in his eyes.

"I am Thor, Odinson, from Asgard. The God of Thunder." Thor squared his shoulders proudly.

"'God of Thunder'? That sounds promising." Grandmaster looked around the room, his guests all nodded in agreement. "Really, I have to see this. Show me the thunder, Thor of Asgard."

Thor gave a defiant look, raised his hand high and closed his eyes. Sparks of electricity began to collect around his hand until a small ball formed. He flung his fist in the direction of the Grandmaster, but it wobbled wildly, hitting one the guests, raising her hair slightly as though she had just experienced a slight jolt of static electricity.

Thor looked at his hand, confused. "It ... it works better with my hammer."

"How many times have we heard that, right?" Grandmaster asked the room, chuckling. "Still, I think with a little snip here and a polish there, I can sell you to the audience."

"What is this audience you keep speaking of?" Thor demanded.

"Oh, just a little thing I like to call the Contest of Champions, the greatest event in the galaxy. And I am the Grandmaster, its highly adored host of the arena and all things on Sakaar. Strange you've never heard of the Contest, though." Grandmaster seemed slightly baffled and mildly offended.

"I've been ... busy," Thor replied, trying not to insult and risk getting shocked again.

"Well, in any case. Two contenders enter the arena, only one exits: the Champion. If you win, you may ask for any wish you desire." Grandmaster had a gleam in his eye. "Right now we're at our highest attendance ever thanks to our current Champion. He's unbeatable. Truly magnificent. You have to meet him." Grandmaster laughed. "What am I saying, of course you'll meet him, just before he probably squashes you. Then again, I don't know how easy Asgardians are to squash. Let me ask ... ah, there he is."

Grandmaster pointed a finger and the crowd of Sakaarian elites parted to reveal ... Loki? The trickster gave a smug look at his brother as he approached.

"Brother? How –?" Thor was thoroughly perplexed at the sight of Loki.

"The same as you, I would gather. Although, I do seem

to appear to have found myself a 'contender' as well. One more in keeping with my own set of skills."

"Brother?" Grandmaster crowed. "Why, how wonderful! Here I am, reuniting families without even realizing it." His cronies all nodded appreciatively at the Grandmaster's unintended kindness.

"You must free me," Thor said urgently to Loki, in a low voice. "Convince this Grandmaster to let me go, then come back with me to Asgard. There is a terrible darkness spreading —" But Thor's pleas fell on deaf ears.

"Back to Asgard? Where no one ever appreciated me for who I really am? I'd rather not, thank you. Especially if there's some 'darkness' overtaking the land." Loki sat on a couch near Thor. "I believe I've finally found my place."

"Your place is with your people," Thor snapped.

Loki grinned, waving an arm across the room. "Exactly. Now, if you want to go back to Asgard, I suggest you work your way home. Go after that wish, and you just might earn it."

"Earning the wish?" Grandmaster's ears perked up. "Well, you'll have to enter the arena as soon as possible, won't you?"

"I'm ready," Thor declared.

Grandmaster looked him up and down. "Mmm, not yet.

Topaz, will you kindly escort our contender to his new home?"

With a look of disdain, Topaz took out an Obedience Disc controller, turned Thor round, and escorted him out of the Grandmaster's chamber, zapping Thor at various intervals.

Thor groaned as his body once again convulsed in the waves of the electric shocks. He suddenly had a feeling that the journey home was going to be far more difficult than he had imagined.

Several moments later, Thor was unceremoniously thrown by an unsmiling Topaz into a dark room in a cavern that ran beneath the surface of Sakaar. The entrance was then sealed by electric bars. Thor looked around, seeing more cells like his lining the tunnels.

"Don't even think of trying to escape," came a voice from the back of his cell. Thor jumped slightly, not realizing he was sharing his cell with another prisoner. He peered in the back corner and a humanoid pile of rocks nearly two metres tall stood and walked towards him.

"You're Kronan, are you not?" Thor had encountered members of his cell-mate's race before.

"Korg. And you're Asgardian. I've heard of you." Korg seemed a quiet soul for such a large presence.

"Are you here to face this 'Champion' as well?" Thor asked.

Korg shook his head no. "I was captured during a revolt against the bounty hunters Grandmaster sends out for the Contest. I had seen many of my kind taken, never to return. When I arrived, I found out why."

"You don't want this wish he's offering? You could end the suffering of your kind."

Korg shook his large head. "I like to live. And as long as I stay here, no other Kronan lives will be taken. So I stick to the undercard, the warm-up before the main event." Korg settled himself back in his corner. "If you're smart, you'll do the same."

Thor steeled his eyes. "I aim to defeat the Champion and earn my way home."

"The only way to do that is to kill him, and that thing is unstoppable. I don't think it can be killed."

Thor turned to face Korg. It was clear he was ready for whatever the Grandmaster could throw at him. "Unkillable?" Thor scoffed. "He clearly has yet to meet me."

CHAPTER 7

Thor spent the entire night awake, unable to think of anything besides facing the Grandmaster's "Champion". Around midday, he and a small band of prisoners were escorted into a large staging area adjacent to the arena. Weapons and armour of all shapes and sizes lined the walls for the would-be fighters to arm themselves with in the coming battles.

As Thor took in his surroundings, he caught sight of a familiar figure. "Valkyrie!" he cried out. Valkyrie turned towards him, another newly acquired prisoner in tow. "Speak with the Grandmaster. Free me and return to save our homeland. For Asgard!"

Valkyrie raised an eyebrow. "You're on Sakaar, not Asgard. Save your pleas for the arena. Not that it'll help much." She turned and started walking away. "Asgard shouldn't hold its breath waiting for your return. You'll be dead soon," she said bluntly, calling over her shoulder.

Thor rolled his eyes at her departure. Not exactly the warm and fuzzy type, then.

As she disappeared round a corner, a loud cheer could be heard coming from the direction of the arena. A moment later Korg came lumbering down the ramp, shield dented, but otherwise unharmed.

"You won, I see?" Thor said, impressed.

"It's why I stay, like I said," Korg replied. He paused in front of Thor for a moment and his eyes grew soft. "I'm sorry for what's about to come. If it means anything, I think you deserve better. Good luck, friend."

Before Thor could reply, a squat alien with an apron came across. He looked the Asgardian over a few times, gave a satisfied grunt and pulled out a razor. Thor raised a fist in opposition, but two guards held him back.

The squat alien motioned to a chair in the corner. "Let's get you ready to fight now."

Without much choice in the matter, Thor sat, but looked on defiantly. "I'm always ready to fight."

The immense octagonal arena was filled to capacity for the day's fight. Hundreds of thousands of spectators, creatures and races that spanned the galaxy, crowded next to each other, their excitement palpable. Above them, ships of all shapes hovered to view the events below. There was never a dull moment in the Grandmaster's Contests, but today the crowd both above and below felt something especially glorious was about to happen. Their beloved Champion was set to fight and from what everyone had heard this would be a match-up for the ages.

At the perfect vantage point was the VIP suite, lavish couches and chairs lining the section. A long golden couch stretched almost the entire length of it. Seated there was the Grandmaster himself. He motioned to Loki, who was mingling among the other guests further inside the suite, indicating the Asgardian should sit near him.

"Shall we start this?" Grandmaster was grinning from ear to ear, rubbing his hands together.

Loki could barely contain his enthusiasm. Finally his arrogant brother would be brought to heel. "To say I've dreamed of a moment like this would be a gross understatement."

"Excellent. Let's give the people what they want, then."

In the centre of the arena, an 18-metre-tall projection

of the Grandmaster suddenly appeared, arms outstretched. "People of Sakaar, travellers, lovers of great sport: welcome to the Contest of Champions, the greatest show in the galaxy!" The crowd roared in excitement. "It's main event time and do I have a show for you. First, your challenger." The response was mixed with both cheers and booing.

The Grandmaster motioned for silence. "Now, now, let's show some sportsmanship. Hailing all the way from Asgard, I present the self-proclaimed God of Thunder, Thor!"

Thor emerged from the shadows, battle ready. His hair was cut close to the scalp, his beard trimmed. He wore armour that resembled that of his Asgardian suit. Strapped to his back were two swords, with a well-worn shield strapped to one arm and a large mace in his other hand. He kicked at the floor, testing the sand and the density. There was no give, so any fall could – would – be brutal.

The crowd erupted at the sight of him. In the seats people were placing bets on how long this newcomer would last. Thor looked around, trying to take in the enormity of his surroundings.

"And the legend that requires no introduction," Grandmaster continued as the doors across the arena began to open slowly. Thor swore he could already hear the creature's breathing through the din of the audience. He placed a helmet on his head and assumed a battle-ready stance, facing the doors.

Grandmaster's projected image gestured towards the opening door. "Your undefeated Champion, the wonder you all come back for time and again, to see him smash his foes. The one, the only, INCREDIBLE –"

An enormous roar split the air, cutting off Grandmaster's introduction. Without waiting for the doors to open completely, a behemoth exploded though the gate, demolishing the entrance. The gigantic green figure was nearly three metres of tall, solid muscle. He wore a Spartan-like helmet, armour covering one shoulder, a battle-axe gripped tightly in one hand and a large war-hammer in the other.

And he was green. Oh so very green.

The audience rose as one to their feet, a deafening cheer filling the arena. The Champion let out a cry that seemed to overwhelm that of the crowd as he beat the war-hammer into the ground. The Grandmaster's projection vanished. Back in his suite, he turned to Loki and smiled.

"A beauty, isn't he?" Grandmaster asked Loki.

For his part, Loki was trying to sink as far down into the lush couch as possible. His face paled.

This "Champion" was no stranger to him. He nodded weakly to Grandmaster in agreement.

In the arena, Thor took in the sight of the Champion and felt the last thing he expected: hope. The figure before him was equally familiar, but unlike with Loki this was a friend. In fact, he would know the creature anywhere, no matter the setting or attire. Before him, the "Champion" was none other than THE HULK!

Thor raised his mace and let out a cry of excitement. The audience quieted, clearly caught off guard by Thor's reaction. Grandmaster looked at Thor quizzically as well.

"I know him!" Thor looked up to Grandmaster's suite, a broad smile crossing his face. "We're friends. From work." He turned back to face the Hulk. "Banner, come, let us team up and –"

Hulk let out another roar at the sound of his alter ego's name. He kicked at the ground like a steed readying itself to charge. He exhaled loudly. Thor began to realize with a heightening sense of dread that there was no look of familiarity in his fellow Avenger's eyes, only a bloodlust. Still, he pushed on, confident there must just be some sort of misunderstanding.

"We needn't fight, Banner. You know me, remember?" Thor's arms were outstretched in a calming manner, but the gesture was lost on Hulk.

"No Banner. Only Hulk!!" he bellowed.

Without warning, Hulk quickly stomped across the arena towards Thor. Thor nimbly flipped over the rampaging beast's back. Hulk stopped and turned.

"I guess reasoning is out of the question here," Thor muttered to himself. He began to twirl his mace as Hulk readied himself for another charge. As the green goliath bounded towards him, Thor hurled his mace directly at Hulk's face. Hulk swatted it away and raised a fist. Thor dodged to the side, barely avoiding being pummelled into the ground.

Thor pulled the two swords from their sheaths on his back and prepared for Hulk's next onslaught. Lifting his war-hammer high, Hulk swung the weapon down. Thor blocked it with the two swords as a loud clank echoed in the arena and the swords broke in two, but Thor was saved. The crowd gasped as one.

Grandmaster turned to Loki. "Your Asgardian comrade is quite impressive, I have to admit."

"He certainly likes to think of himself as such," Loki said, rolling his eyes.

Hulk began twirling his battle-axe and war-hammer in an intricate and deadly pattern. Thor tossed aside the now-broken swords and backed away, watching the timing, searching for an opening. This time, he swiftly lunged at the oncoming Hulk and stopped the war-hammer with his shield. The weapon flew out of the Hulk's hand. A punch to the arm caused Hulk to drop the battle-axe. Thor kicked his enraged opponent away, and the two rolled to opposite ends of the arena.

"Hulk! We are friends!" Thor called out across the arena. "We need not entertain this any longer!"

The crowd booed Thor's attempt to cease the Contest and began to chant "CHAMPION!" over and over. Hulk lowered his head, preparing to charge. Thor crouched in a runner's stance, at the ready to meet in the middle.

The two friends-turned-opponents sprinted towards each other. Just as they reached the middle, Hulk leaped up, both fists raised high. Thor, anticipating this approach, timed his jump so he was just under Hulk as he left the ground. A powerful uppercut from Thor connected with Hulk's jaw and the crowd gasped as the blow knocked the helmet off their Champion's head.

With the Hulk caught off-guard, Thor began to land blow after blow on his big green head. Hulk began to swing wildly, missing each time as every punch thrown by Thor landed, knocking the Champion more and more off balance. Thor could feel Hulk weakening, and even as he wanted to stop and force Hulk to recognize him as his friend, not his adversary, Thor knew he had to keep going so he could win the Contest and get his wish, and get home to Asgard.

Suddenly, a jolt of electricity shot through Thor. He fell to the ground, writhing in pain, his stride broken. Looking towards the Grandmaster's suite, he saw the man hold up a control in one hand as he waved his finger back and forth.

It was the Obedience Disc.

Seizing upon Thor's moment of weakness, Hulk grabbed the thunder god by his feet and began to swing him back and forth, slamming Thor into the ground left and right and left and right. Loki, having been on the receiving end of this move before, stifled a grin in the VIP suite.

Thor lay on the ground of the arena, bloodied and bruised. He watched in paralysed pain as Hulk launched himself in the air, nearly as high as the ships hovering above. The brute began his descent, fists first. At the last possible second, Thor rolled clear, a breath away from being smashed to a probable death.

"Hulk," Thor gasped, "Banner, remember who you are. We are friends."

Hulk paused for a moment. "Friends?"

Grandmaster stood with the rest of the audience, clapping, cheering for his Champion to deliver the final blow. But Hulk looked at Thor, helpless in the sand at his feet.

"Yes... friends. Hulk and Thor." The Asgardian begged the fates for his words to get through to the Hulk.

Hulk reached down and grabbed Thor by the chest.

"Friend," he whispered into Thor's ear, right before he hurled Thor back down one final time, and the last thing Thor saw was the floor of the arena rising up to meet him just before everything went black.

CHAPTER 8

The dull roar in his ears certainly wasn't the audience, that much Thor knew. How long he had been out was a different question entirely. As was the question of where he currently was. As he drifted in and out of consciousness, his eyes began to take in the room around him. He was laid out on a soft leather sofa built for someone of a much greater size than him. There was thick-looking carpeting lining the floors, and lush red velvet curtains that blocked out any light that might try to filter through. A massive four-poster bed sat in one corner of the room. As the roaring in his head died down, Thor thought he could hear bubbles. Maybe he was suffering from a concussion.

But then, turning his head, Thor witnessed a sight he never thought he would behold: Hulk lounging in a natural hot spring as though it was a hot tub, emitting a moan of deep and appreciative pleasure as the soothing water relaxed his battle-weary muscles.

"Where am I?" Thor asked.

"Hulk home. Thor friend. Friend rest." Hulk rattled off the statements as facts, with no room to argue. Not that Thor would. He knew how close he had come to dying in that arena. Grandmaster's meddling had nearly cost Thor his life. Fortunately, Thor realized he had been able to get through to his friend. Hulk had somehow managed to save Thor from total obliteration, and that meant some semblance of Banner clung to this battling Champion. Thor felt the small spark of hope flare once again.

"Hulk. Thank you for sparing me. We are alone, yes?" Hulk nodded. "May I speak with Banner?"

Hulk stirred in the spring, his brow furrowing. "No Banner, only Hulk."

His tone told Thor not to push the matter at the moment. "Very well. Good to know. How did you get here? How long have you been on this planet, Hulk?"

The look on Hulk's face changed to one of confusion. "Hulk not know. A ship, then Hulk here. Hulk fight. Hulk win."

Thor's heart sank. The ship, it must have been the

Quinjet, which Banner had left on after the Battle of Sokovia. He'd turned off his comm, and that was the last the Avengers had heard of him ... until now. Had his friend been here all these years since?

"Hulk ... we tried tracking you, all of us, to bring you home," Thor began carefully.

But Hulk ignored him, standing up and splashing water everywhere as he climbed out of the springs, dried and began to dress for battle; a newly repaired helmet hung alongside a wall of weapons.

"Hulk home now." He sounded resigned to the fact and even happy about it, or as happy as Hulk could get.

"It doesn't have to be. We can leave here. Together! Please, Hulk, my home, Asagard, it ... it needs me. Now more than ever. And with your strength, I could really use you there with me."

Hulk had finished dressing. "Hulk home. Thor friend. Thor stay."

Thor warily got to his feet. "Hulk, please. At least release me. Convince the Grandmaster to set me free so I can leave and —"

Thor suddenly found himself face-to-face with the Hulk, his large green eyes narrowed. "Thor friend. Thor stay."

The tiniest of taps from Hulk put Thor back on the oversized lounge.

As Hulk exited his chamber, Thor gave a weak wave. "Stay alive. Although you seem to be doing a fairly good job at that," he muttered as his friend and saviour left.

Thor waited until he could hear the uproarious cheering of the crowd far in the distance as their "Champion" entered the arena. He creeped to the door and looked round. The coast was clear. He went to the wall and chose a nasty-looking spiked ball-and-chain and headed towards the exit. As soon as he passed completely through it, however, his body was hit with a massive jolt of electricity that sent him reeling. He tried to walk forward but the pain from the Obedience Disc was too much and he collapsed, falling back into the Hulk's suite.

"Plan ... B?" Thor wondered aloud as he fell to the ground, losing consciousness once again.

He came to a little while later, finding himself back on the luxurious sofa. Thor saw Hulk pacing the room. "Congratulations, I assume?" Thor asked mildly.

Hearing Thor awake, Hulk marched over to him and pointed at the Obedience Disc. "Thor friend. Friend stay!"

"Yes, yes, I know. 'Hulk home', doesn't want to leave; we've tried that route." Thor's mind raced. He knew there had to be a way out. Looking towards the door, he smiled. *Of course*, he thought, *the way out is quite often the way in*. An idea quickly formed.

"Hulk, Thor friend, yes?" Hulk nodded. "What if I told you I had a friend here, someone I would very much like to see. Could you get them for me? As a favour?"

"Thor stay?" Hulk sounded hesitant.

Thor nodded. "Yes, Thor stay. Right here until you return."

With that, Thor began to tell Hulk who he needed to see and how to find them.

"You MUST be kidding me with this."

Thor turned at the sound of the voice coming from the entrance. It was Valkyrie! Hulk walked in past her and plopped himself on the large sofa.

"Thor friend," he said to Valkyrie by way of explanation.

"Not one of mine," she answered, and turned to leave.

"Wait!" Thor cried out. "Before I fell off the Bifrost, in the darkness that was consuming it, I feel like I may have seen something ... a woman. She has been plaguing my nightmares and now I fear she has Asgard in her grasp."

Valkyrie stopped at Thor's revelation. She shook her head as she turned. "Where is Odin? Shouldn't he be protecting his kingdom?"

"He ... I don't know. He's not on Asgard, though." Thor moved towards her, taking hold of her arm. "You know something, don't you?"

"That you don't know or haven't figured it out shows how much Odin has prepared his heir. And what little he cares of the other Valkyries after...." Her voice trailed off.

"What? After what? Tell me so I can fix whatever it is my father has failed to."

Valkyrie's eyes flashed in anger. "That was our job! Odin tasked the Valkyries to drive back what has returned."

"And that is?" Thor was anxious. The answer was near.

"Hela." Valkyrie spat the name out. "Goddess of the Dead, ruler of Hel. She was one of Odin's mistakes. His biggest, if you ask me. We fought hard to drive her back and a curse was placed on her: as long as Odin sits on the throne, Asgard would be safe from her."

Thor's head fell. "And because of my brother's manipulations, Odin was dethroned and wandering Midgard for some time."

"Giving Hela the time and opportunity she needed.

To raise an attack." She patted Thor on the shoulder. "Sorry, but Asgard's doomed and there's nothing you can do about it."

Thor's eyes lit up. "There is a way off this world. I know how; I just don't know where. The vessel that brought my friend here, do you know where it is?"

Valkyrie shrugged. "Probably in the old shipyard near the marketplace. Not that it'll do you any good. It's not like you're going anywhere."

Thor suddenly grinned and squeezed Valkyrie in a tight hug, prompting a sound of disgust from her as she pushed him away and stomped towards the door. He kept walking after her, backwards through the door. Hulk had nodded off during their conversation. Thor gave a silent wave to his sleeping friend and walked through the doorway, unharmed.

Valkyrie was stunned. "How –?"

Thor held up the Obedience Disc controller that he had lifted off her when he'd given her a hug. He'd used the controller to disable the Obedience Disc on his chest, which no longer glowed. He reached for it and popped it off his chest, slipping it into his belt. With that, he turned and raced out of the suite, leaving a speechless Valkyrie and a snoring Hulk behind.

CHAPTER 9

The shipyard looked like the galaxy's version of a used car lot. Ships of all sizes and conditions were piled two- or three-deep, some on top of others, rusting away. Thor darted in and out of the rows until....

There!

He ran to a familiar-looking ship. It was slightly dusty but looked to be in one piece. "I could kiss you," he happily told the Quinjet, the same ship that had brought Hulk to the planet.

He climbed into the cockpit and searched for the controls to turn it on. A voice suddenly came from the speakers. "Please speak the activation code."

"Yes!" Thor exclaimed. "Ummm, let's try 'Avengers Assemble'."

"I'm sorry, that is incorrect," the ship replied.

Thor wracked his brain. What would Tony Stark have programmed into this? Sighing, he tried again. "Tony Stark is a genius."

The Quinjet's control board lit up. "Activation code accepted."

Thor laughed at his good fortune. He reached to fire up the engines when suddenly he heard a *RIIIIIIP* from the back of the ship. Turning he saw that the Hulk had followed him to the shipyard and was now in the process of tearing off the back end of the Quinjet.

"Thor friend, Thor stay!" Hulk roared at him.

Before Thor could respond, the Quinjet, lights flickering, spoke once more. "Voice recognition. Bruce Banner, Hulk. Message retrieval activated."

Thor looked at the controls as a familiar face appeared on the screen: it was Natasha Romanov, also known as Black Widow. She and Hulk had been close friends back when Hulk was still on Earth, fighting alongside the Avengers.

"Hey, big guy," she began haltingly, her features sad and worried. "Not sure if you're out there. Not sure if you're even getting these. Fifth I've sent so far. I know you must be scared out there, wherever you are. But everything will be fine." The screen flickered for a moment and Black Widow reappeared. "I miss you. And the sun's getting real low...."

The image faded as the message ended. Thor turned. Hulk's gaze was transfixed on the screen. He reached out to touch it and as he did so, his arm began to shrink, along with his entire body.

Slowly, the Hulk transformed back into Bruce Banner.

Thor raced to embrace his friend. "She encoded a trigger phrase! Brilliant work – I wish I knew about that one. It would have saved a beating and a lot of hurt. But welcome back!"

Bruce was in a state of shock. He pushed out of Thor's friendly embrace and looked around wildly. "Where-where am I?" Memories began to come racing back and he began to panic. "Ultron! Sokovia! We have to stop him. I didn't want to harm anyone else, I wanted to –"

Thor tried to calm Banner. "My friend, please. Listen to me. Ultron was defeated. The Avengers destroyed him."

"When? How?" Banner was baffled.

"Two years ago." Thor sighed, hating to deliver the news.

Banner's eyes widened. "Two – two YEARS?" Looking around, he took in the alien sights and sounds. Turning to Thor, a terrified look crossed his features. "Hulk. He's been in control this whole time. Do I even want to know what he's been doing?"

"Probably best you don't. Let's just say you're quite popular here, and very recognizable, so try to remain calm and in control."

"Says the God of Thunder." Banner's voice was tinged with panic as he tried to breathe.

"Not so much on this world."

Banner looked to Thor, desperation in his eyes. "So, what's the plan? How do we get out of here and back home?"

Thor nodded to the Quinjet, which was now torn in two. "Well, our first option is off the table. But I know someone who might be able to help."

"You've lost them BOTH? The blond one I can kind of understand, but the Champion, too? How do you lose a two-ton green killing monster?!"

Valkyrie winced as Grandmaster's tirade continued. Grandmaster, for his part, tried to calm himself as he paced his chamber. "Think, think, think. Ah! A game!"

"Game?" Valkyrie raised an eyebrow. Now did not

seem the time for games.

"A contest. See who can find them first. You, or ..." he turned to face Loki, seated comfortably in the corner. "His brother."

Loki appeared taken aback. "Me? Whatever for? Games are my forte, but not these sorts. Mine are more ... cerebral, shall we say?"

"You are related, you know how he thinks. And," Grandmaster paused, a gleam in his eye. "You love money."

This piqued both Valkyrie and Loki's interests. "How much are we talking?" Valkyrie asked.

"More than you've ever been paid. Combined." Grandmaster's face turned serious. "The first of you to find my Champion and return him to me wins. As for the Asgardian, do whatever you want with him. He's too much trouble as it is."

Valkyrie and Loki eyed each other, sizing up the competition. "What are you waiting for? Go!" Grandmaster ordered. With that, the contest was on between the two new rivals.

"This is insane, you know that, right?" Banner was racing to keep up with Thor. He was wearing new clothes found in an emergency compartment in the Quinjet: jeans and a T-shirt that read 'Stark Rules'.

"The situation is a bit dire, I'll give you that," Thor replied.

"I meant all of this." Bruce gestured widely to emphasize his point.

The two were racing through the streets of the marketplace. Everywhere there were vendors selling "Champion" merchandise. Hulk masks, shirts and fists that roared when punched together.

"I told you, he's quite popular here." Thor led them out of the market and accidentally straight into a parade celebrating the Champion. A band was playing and green powder exploded everywhere.

One parade-goer pointed what looked like a party popper at Bruce's face, pulled a string and *POP!* Bruce was covered in the green powder.

Bruce could feel himself starting to lose control in the face of all this Hulk-mania. He fought for calm. "The sun's getting real low ... the sun's getting real low," Bruce repeated as he stumbled through the crowd, blinded by the powder. He crashed into a rather unpleasant-looking alien who immediately took offence. Bruce looked around, but he had lost Thor in the crowd. The angered alien began to

raise his fist, ready to pummel Bruce when ... *ZZZZZZAP!*
He began to shake uncontrollably and fell face down.

Bruce examined the alien and saw an Obedience Disc
attached to his back. "You're new," came a voice from
behind him.

Bruce turned and saw Valkyrie. She was holding the
control for the Obedience Disc in her hand as she looked
him over. "Too bad you're of no use to me. You wouldn't
last five seconds in the arena."

"You have no idea how wrong you are," Thor said,
pushing his way to them.

"Arena? What arena?" Bruce's confusion was
compounded the longer he stayed, he realized.

"Valkyrie, meet your Champion." Thor motioned
towards the baffled Bruce.

Valkyrie looked stunned at the sight of the once
unstoppable force of nature reduced to this human
standing before her. "This? But he's so ..." she wrinkled
her nose, "... puny."

Banner stood a little taller, taking offence. "I prefer the
term 'academic'."

Thor moved to Valkyrie. "I've been searching for you."

"I was about to say the same thing," she replied.

"Please. Tell me you're here to help," Thor's said.

Valkyrie scoffed and motioned for the pair to follow her. She shook her head. "You're persistent, I'll give you that. Thick-headed, but persistent."

CHAPTER 10

The trio made their way through the parade, dodging and weaving through overly enthusiastic partiers all celebrating the Hulk's triumphs. Bruce still couldn't believe there was a place where his destructive alter ego could be so celebrated.

"So, how do you two know each other?" he yelled to Valkyrie and Thor above the din of the revellers.

"She is a great warrior of Asgard lore," Thor said.

"He was my prisoner," overlapped Valkyrie. "I brought him to fight you."

Banner was taken aback. "We ... fought?" His eyes grew wide with dread. "Did I hurt you?"

Thor waved away his friend's concerns. "Nothing time and maybe some healing waters and fine wine in Asgard can't cure."

Valkyrie smiled at the notion Bruce was unaware of his actions as the Hulk. "He's lucky you two are friends," she told him. "You've been the Champion for a while for a reason."

Banner seemed despondent. "This celebration, these people, they adore the Hulk. What did I do to deserve this?"

"Well, you managed to successfully ki–"

Thor interrupted Valkyrie, desperate to change the subject. "Where are we going?"

"My ship. The Grandmaster wants you, and I'm turning down a lot of money for doing this, so piss me off and I might change my mind." Valkyrie's tone had changed since they'd last spoken, Thor noticed.

"Why the change of heart?" Thor was genuinely curious.

A sigh came from Valkyrie. "Hela. You had to go and tell me she was back." The warrior shook her head. "It is a Valkyrie's duty to protect Asgard from her. When she attacked before, I was too young and naïve to think I could handle her on my own." She paused, remembering her past. "I didn't last beyond the first wave of her attack."

"So you'll return with me to Asgard and finish what

you started?" Thor was pleased he had finally got through to her.

"I'll do what I can to get you to Asgard. THEN we'll see what I do." Valkyrie motioned for them to follow her. "We're here."

Thor recognized the sleek vessel from earlier, when she'd first captured him to deliver him to the Grandmaster. Valkyrie's ship was clearly one of the finer pieces of machinery flying the Sakaarian skies. The three boarded the ship.

"You'll need to sit up here with me. We have company in the back." Valkyrie turned their attention to a bound and gagged figure in the rear of the ship. It was Loki. Thor immediately grabbed the nearest object, a wrench, and threw it at his brother. The wrench hit Loki squarely in the chest and he let out a muffled cry.

"I had to be sure," Thor explained. "He's known for his illusions."

"I had to be sure he wouldn't beat me in the Grandmaster's bet in case he found you first and took you to the crazy fool like the lapdog he's become." Valkyrie clearly had no patience for the trickster.

Thor chuckled. "You've come to know my brother well."

"Loki's here? Are you guys insane? Don't you remember what he did to us all the last time?" Bruce was eyeing the tied-up villain warily.

"Yes, and I'm sure he remembers who it was that helped put an end to his mad quest. If he moves, feel free to go green on him again." Thor smiled as Loki visibly paled at the memory.

Valkyrie was punching coordinates into her navigation system. "I figure our best bet is to get to Xandar, refuel and stock up on supplies. If we maintain top speed we should reach Asgard in eighteen months or so."

Thor was aghast. "EIGHTEEN MONTHS? Asgard may not even have eighteen hours if Hela has truly returned and is as deadly as you say!"

"I'm the one with the ship, but I'm open to suggestions." Valkyrie sat back, confident that hers was the best option.

"Is there a faster ship?" Valkyrie shook her head. Thor scanned the sky, looking at the many wormholes. "We came here through one of those. Perhaps we can return the same way."

Valkyrie laughed in his face. "Okay, thunder god. Pick one and I'll tell you how that won't work."

He pointed at the vast wormhole that took up nearly a third of the sky. "That one. It seems like it could lead us wherever we need to be in the shortest amount of time."

Slackjawed, Valkyrie gazed at Thor in silence for a moment before bursting into a fit of hysterics. "You expect me to fly into the Magnetar? This ship wouldn't last a minute in there, and I didn't sign up for a suicide run."

Banner pushed his way into the cockpit to get a better view. "You have a Magnetar wormhole here?"

"You know of this?" Thor asked.

"I studied it as part of my fourth doctorate."

"Then you can help us navigate through it. Perfect!" Thor beamed.

Bruce didn't look as convinced. "I don't think you understand. The interior of a Magnetar wormhole is such that even a teaspoon of its atmosphere would have the mass of a hundred million tons."

Thor looked at his friend, not grasping the issue. "Sooo...."

"We drink and toast to an impossible plan," Valkyrie answered.

"Surely there is a way, Banner." Thor was insistent.

Bruce thought for a moment. "Well, assuming none of us black out during the journey from the pressure, then we would still need a ship that could withstand the geodetic strain of the wormhole without shields, AND some kind of offline power-steering mechanism that could function without the onboard computer system."

Valkyrie stared at Bruce. "You're right. Academic suits you better than puny."

"Can we find such a vessel here?" Thor asked.

A series of muffled grunts and sounds came from the back. They turned to see Loki trying to spit out his gag. Thor cautiously approached his brother and took off the binding round his mouth.

"Finally. Thank you. If you had let me join the conversation earlier, I could have avoided Doctor Banner's physics lesson." Thor moved to replace the gag but Loki dodged him. "Apologies. One tends to get a bit testy when tied up in the back of a strange ship and having tools tossed at him."

"You said you had a solution? Spit it out." Thor's patience was running thin.

"Grandmaster gave me a tour of his palace and he has a collection of only the finest ships in the galaxy in his garage."

"So we hotwire a ship from the guy that's held me hostage for two years?" Bruce asked incredulously.

"Have you a better idea?" Loki retorted.

Bruce shook his head. "Just making sure we were

screwing over the right guy."

Loki turned back to Thor. "Free me, brother, and I can lead you to where he stores his ships. I have studied his compound and am certain we can easily evade detection and find the ship we need." Loki looked and sounded sincere. Thor paused a moment before unbinding his brother.

The unlikely pair began to exit the ship before Thor paused, looking back to Valkyrie. "For this to work, I think it best if we have some sort of distraction."

A grin crossed Valkyrie's face. "I think I know just the thing."

As Loki and Thor exited the ship, Valkyrie lifted off and headed towards the arena.

Thor looked at his brother. "We'll only have one chance at this. Do not mess it up."

Loki gave a grin. "Trust me, brother. I have everything under control."

Bruce watched as Valkyrie landed her ship in the middle of the arena. "What are you planning?"

"If I were you, I'd worry less about that and more about staying small and pink." Valkyrie smiled. "Everyone out there might love the Champion, but these guys may not be so happy to see Big Green. You're their main competition."

Banner waited in the ship as Valkyrie easily took out two guards stationed in front of a dark cavern. Within moments, he began to hear an approaching roar and felt the ground shake. Valkyrie came bolting out of the entrance to the cavern. Bruce couldn't believe his eyes when he saw what followed her.

Dozens of aliens came pouring out of the cavern. Weapons were being passed around to each as the freed prisoners armed themselves. Valkyrie's ship began its ascent and she and Bruce flew over Korg, who had taken control of the freed prisoners and was readying the group for battle.

Valkyrie flipped a switch and a loudspeaker projected her voice to the crowd below. Looking at Korg, she said, "The God of Thunder sends his best."

With that, she flew off as a full-scale riot began.

CHAPTER 11

"Can anyone please explain to me how things got to this point?" Grandmaster demanded as he made his way through the hallways of his massive ship. Looking down on to the dismal scene below, he saw his finest fighters he had been grooming for his beloved Contests inciting a riot, running through the streets, destroying anything that bore the Champion's face.

A guard approached the Grandmaster. "Well, sir, the slaves —"

Grandmaster cut him off with a glare. "What have I said about that word?"

The guard, chagrined, corrected himself. "The 'prisoners with jobs' were freed, it appears, by Scrapper 142."

Topaz snorted from behind the Grandmaster. "Figures. I told you she couldn't be trusted," she said smugly.

"Now, now. This is not the time for petty jealousies. We need constructive criticism. And a plan. An extra week's pay for the person who comes up with the best plan. Go!" Grandmaster settled himself in a plush captain's chair in the deck of the ship and watched as his city erupted into chaos. His ship was soon flanked by half a dozen warships that meant to end this riot, and quickly.

Below, Korg looked up to see the man who had pillaged his beloved city for sport. His chance for redemption, and to complete the uprising he'd once been a part of, was finally at hand. With a cry, he directed his fellow freed fighters to focus their attacks towards the ship. Grandmaster's vessel was suddenly bombarded with blasts, rocks and anything the rioters could throw or fire at it.

Growing more agitated, Grandmaster repeated wildly, "The plan? Anyone?!"

"What *is* your plan here, brother?" Thor whispered as the two skulked quietly through the depths of the Grandmaster's palace.

"Patience, dear brother. First we must worry about the

two guards blocking our path."

Acting in tandem, the sons of Odin disarmed the guards and knocked them unconscious with one fluid movement.

"You'll help us free Asgard from Hela's grip when we arrive? I can count on you?" Thor asked.

"Of course. After all, I'm sure you blame me for her resurgence. It's the least I can do." Loki appeared contrite. "Although I am curious, why the sudden change of heart to become Odinson and assume the throne?"

"It is what is needed to defeat Hela, therefore it is my duty," Thor said plainly. He let out a small sigh, his voice almost apologetic. "In the past I demanded the throne when I hadn't earned it, and then refused the throne when Asgard needed me most. You stole it. Twice."

"Yet you are always forgiven," Loki said, trying not to sneer.

"My point is that our self-centred conflict over Asgard has ruined our kingdom. We have been so focused on fighting for the top, we've forgotten there's a middle and a bottom. If I'm to be king, then I want to be a custodian, not a conqueror."

"Why the sudden baring of your soul to me?" Loki asked.

Thor turned to his brother. "Because I want to change.

I want to be better. And I think you can, too. Helping us escape has shown you can take strides towards that." He looked at Loki earnestly. "Make a fresh start, brother. It's time."

Grandmaster was at his wit's end. Never had he thought a day like this would come. All he'd worked for was vanishing before his eyes. Talking into the communications system's microphone, his voice was broadcast to those below.

"If you force me to kill you, then I won't have anyone for next week's fight! Can't we reach some sort of compromise? You, Korg, talk some sense into this mob." Grandmaster flopped back into his chair, hoping his words got through to the protesters.

Below, Korg picked up a vendor's cart full of Champion flags and hurled it at Grandmaster's ship. Grandmaster sighed heavily. "So much for reason." He turned to a soldier stationed at a weapon control centre and gave him a wave.

The ship's turrets turned to aim below. Gas began to leak out as Grandmaster unleashed a chemical into the air. Korg covered his face and urged everyone to take cover as the fighting began to escalate.

CHAPTER 12

The brothers finally reached Grandmaster's garage. Before them was a vast array of ships from across the galaxy. Dozens lined the walls. Thor began to examine each one.

"If I may," Loki spoke up, "the Grandmaster's personal limousine is quite remarkable. A thing of beauty, really. He showed me the city in it when I first arrived."

"I doubt a luxury vehicle is what Banner called for," Thor answered.

"A shame. I would love to have one as my own."

Thor sighed, "I'm sure you would, brother. Will you at least start looking for anything resembling Banner's description?"

Loki laughed. "I merely said I could possibly show you where to find what you were looking for. I didn't actually grasp a word he was babbling about."

"No matter, I think this may be exactly what we need." Thor stopped in front of a ship unlike any he had ever seen before. It was glorious. Sleek yet sturdy, clearly top-of-the-line technology. The cockpit had more controls than Thor had ever seen in his life, even more advanced than something Tony Stark could possibly design. Probably.

"Ah, the Commodore. You have excellent taste, brother. Grandmaster bragged about this one, calling it his newest acquisition."

"It is our acquisition now. Come, Valkyrie must be ready for us."

Thor and Loki quickly boarded the swift ship as the noise of the riots grew louder in the distance.

"Here they come," Valkyrie said, her voice tinged with envy. "Loki wasn't kidding. Grandmaster has some beauties when it comes to ships."

"Speaking of," Bruce said, pointing. "Incoming."

"I saw that one five seconds ago. I was waiting for it to get in range." She blasted the oncoming warship while still looking at Bruce.

"Show off." Bruce had to admit, he was rather impressed

by her skills as a warrior and pilot.

The comms crackled on in the ship. "Commodore to Valkyrie, do you copy?"

"Listen to you. Thor steals one ship and suddenly he starts talking like a pilot." Valkyrie gave a slight grin of approval.

"In case you hadn't noticed, your little 'distraction' has turned into an all-out war," came Thor's voice over the comm.

Valkyrie sat back, satisfied, taking it all in. "I know. Isn't it great?"

"Not the words I'd choose, considering we have another war to fight. I'd rather we exit this one as soon as possible." Thor did not sound amused. "Banner, will this ship suffice to make it through your wormhole?"

"I wouldn't exactly claim it as mine, but it looks sturdy. I'll need a closer examination to determine exactly —"

Bruce was cut off by Valkyrie. "Thor, do you know how to open the bay doors?"

"I believe so, yes. Why?" he replied.

"Open them up." She turned to Bruce. "I wanna make sure we survive this insane gambit of yours. So, you need a better look? No time like the present." Valkyrie flipped the ship in mid-air, pushed a button on the dash, and Bruce was suddenly ejected from the ship.

Bruce let out a scream as he descended, trying desperately not to transform into the Hulk out of fear. At the last second, the Commodore was under him, bay doors open. Banner fell through them and somehow landed softly in a cushioned chair.

"Anti-grav stabilizing interior atmosphere. This *is* an impressive ship." He was pleased, both by the ship and that he'd survived his "fall" from Valkyrie's ship.

"Excellent, now can you please examine the rest for our safe passage?" Thor was beginning to lose patience.

As Bruce looked over the ship's schematics, Thor searched the skies for Valkyrie's ship. He watched as she dodged and weaved through the warships.

At last, Bruce gave a nod. "Seems like this should work. In theory."

"Good enough for me. Valkyrie, we are all clear. Prepare to board," Thor radioed.

"One sec," Valkyrie's voice came over the comms. "I have one last score to settle."

Bruce looked to the back of the Commodore and saw Loki. "He's still with us?"

"On surprisingly good behaviour. He's probably worried about our green friend reappearing and knocking him about again," Thor responded. He watched as Valkyrie aimed her ship directly at the Grandmaster's. "Insane woman, what is she thinking?"

As if to answer his question, Valkyrie's ship's booster engines fired, speeding up her ship for a direct collision course with the cockpit of the Grandmaster's. Thor watched in horror as Valkyrie's ship smashed into Grandmaster in a fireball of an explosion.

"NO!" Thor exclaimed. His face looked stricken. Why would she sacrifice herself after all this? What had she been thinking?

"Wait, look." Bruce pointed. A small figure was heading straight towards them, flipping in mid-air as it descended. As the figure approached them at rapid-fire speed, Thor heaved a sigh of relief. It was Valkyrie!

She landed on the Commodore's windshield, standing upright. "Room for one more?" she quipped.

Thor opened the bay door and Valkyrie boarded the ship. "Scoot over, thunder god. We're going to need a real pilot."

Taking control of the ship's steering, Valkyrie smiled. "Now *this* is the kind of ship I was born to fly. Hold on, boys." She fired and revved up the engines, increasing the speed to maximum velocity. Behind them, the remaining warships followed, firing on the vessel, which Valkyrie easily evaded.

She pulled the controls towards her and the ship angled up. It began to climb higher and higher into the atmosphere. The warships peeled off, not built for the heightening altitude nor willing to follow the Commodore's flight path.

After all, it was heading straight for the Magnetar.

As they grew closer, debris whipped around them at crushing speeds. Lightning crashed in front of the ship as massive storms brewed on all sides. But Valkyrie expertly avoided everything the Magnetar was throwing at them.

"Last chance to back out. Anyone? Maybe eject the mischief-maker back there?" Valkyrie said, her face serious.

"Where I go, he goes. He must face what he has brought upon our home," Thor replied.

"Buckle in, because this might not be pretty." Valkyrie stared at the heart of the wormhole.

Thor and Bruce locked eyes for a moment in mutual agreement before Thor turned his gaze forward, his face set for what was to come. "For the glory of Asgard." Valkyrie glanced over at him and Thor met her look. She gave a simple nod. She was ready.

Thor stared into the wormhole and braced himself,

both for the flight they were about to embark on to reach Asgard and the battle they would surely face once they got there. He knew he was ready. Ready for Hela. Ready for the fight.

And, most important, ready for the throne.

He gave a small smile as Valkyrie engaged the thrusters to full speed and the Commodore vanished into the wormhole.

Thor was finally going home.